ONE FINE DAY

ONE FINE DAY
JOHN QUINN

For Donna

Happy Reading!

Best Wishes

John Quinn

Published 1996
by Poolbeg Press Ltd
123 Baldoyle Industrial Estate
Dublin 13, Ireland

© John Quinn 1996

The moral right of the author has been asserted.

The Publishers gratefully acknowledge the support of The Arts Council.

A catalogue record for this book is available from the British Library.

ISBN 1 85371 612 X

Cover illustration by Moira MacNamara
Cover design by Poolbeg Group Services Ltd
Set by Poolbeg Group Services Ltd in Garamond 10.5/14
Printed by The Guernsey Press Ltd,
Vale, Guernsey, Channel Islands.

About the Author

John Quinn has been a broadcaster for twenty years. As a radio producer with RTE his programmes have been acclaimed at home and abroad.

His highly popular children's novels include *Duck and Swan, The Gold Cross of Killadoo* and *The Summer of Lily and Esme* which won the Bisto Book of the Year Award in 1992.

Also by John Quinn

The Gold Cross of Killadoo

The Summer of Lily and Esme

Duck and Swan

Published by Poolbeg

For Lorraine and Kiran

with admiration

Uno speciale ringraziamento

a Silvia

Un bel di vedremo
levarsi un fil di fumo
Sull' estremo confin del mare,
E poi la nave appare . . .

One fine day we'll see
a wisp of smoke rising
from the distant horizon of the sea.
And then the ship will appear . . .

(*Giacomo Puccini* / Madama Butterfly)

Chapter One

He hated the sound of breaking glass. It kept recurring in the nightmare. Always the same nightmare. A girl on a bicycle. She leans the bicycle against the shop window. Then the car-bomb. The shop window explodes. An ear-splitting crack as the plate-glass shatters into jagged vicious shards. One of them spears the girl in the chest. Silence. Then screams. Alarms. Sirens. Footsteps running in panic. Confusion. But through it all the shattering glass echoes, re-echoes, re-echoes . . .

"Rossa! For Christ's sake, get out! Get out!" His mother stood in the doorway, clutching a terrified James in front of her. It wasn't a nightmare. Another window shattered downstairs. "Get out quick. They're going to burn us out for sure!" She clasped James even more tightly to her as she gave an anxious glance down the stairs to the front door. "Just grab a few clothes and come on!" Rossa leaped out of bed and dressed very quickly. He could only find one boot. "Rossa, come on!" There was growing panic in his mother's voice.

"I'm coming! I'm coming. Can't find my bloody – "

1

There it was. Under the bed. As he pulled it on with one hand he peered through a chink in the curtain.

A cluster of eight or ten youths paced up and down on the roadway outside. A few of them wearing balaclavas crouched in a huddle behind a car. The others hurled stones, then paused to chant in unison:

"Provos out! Kill the Fenian butchers! Provos out!"

Fear froze his body. The nightmare grew more real with each chant.

"Rossa!" His mother's terrified scream unlocked his body.

"I'm comin', I'm comin'." He let go of the curtain and hastily tied his bootlaces. Jacket. Where's my leather jacket? He tore the clothes from the wardrobe until he found the jacket. He groped along the top of the wardrobe until his fingers touched the biscuit tin. He grabbed it, shoved it inside his jacket and made for the door. On an impulse he turned back to the window. He made a chink in the curtain and peered through. It was as if he were still trying to convince himself that this was all unreal. Maybe this time he would see only the black night, just the outline of a few cars parked under the broken street-light. And then he would wake up . . .

The gloom outside was lit up by an eerie glow. The group huddled behind the car were now standing up. Four of them, each of their masked faces weirdly lit by the dancing flames of the petrol bombs they held aloft momentarily. And then in unison they hurled the bombs in different directions. One of them spiralled upwards towards Rossa's window. He watched, disbelieving, as the flaming bottle sailed towards him – in slow motion, it seemed.

At the last moment he drew the curtains tightly shut. The window shattered. He hated the sound of breaking glass . . . He cupped his hands around his ears and stood terrified as spatters of flame hooked themselves onto the curtains. A great cheer went up on the roadway. The chanting resumed:

"Provos out! Fenian butchers!"

His mother's voice pierced the entire din outside.

"Rossa! Jesus Christ!"

The curtains were on fire. He turned and ran, clearing the stairs in four leaps.

"James! Help me with James!" his mother pleaded. James clung fiercely to the banister. His mother could not prise the boy's hands open.

"Come on, James," Rossa cried. "We have to go." He tore at his brother's hands but they were solidly locked together.

"Fire, James!" Rossa screamed. "The house is on fire."

James shook his head rapidly.

"Bin! Bin! Bin! Bin!" he repeated in a strangely calm voice.

Ross looked at his mother.

"Under the stairs," she whispered.

Rossa slammed back the latch on the door of the stair cupboard. He grabbed the black rubbish bin and tore off the lid.

"In!" he barked.

James clambered into the bin.

"Sit down, will you?"

James began shaking his head again.

"Rocky. Rocky. Rocky," he said.

"Ah Jesus!" Rossa exclaimed. He raced into the kitchen

and grabbed the terrapin tank from a shelf. He thrust it into James's outstretched arms and forcibly squashed his brother down into the bin, slammed the lid and took it up by the handles. As he struggled towards the front door he could hear the water from the tank slosh around inside the bin.

"Serves you right if you bloody drown in there!" he muttered.

His mother took a firm grip on a bulging refuse sack and paused before opening the door.

"Can you manage him?" she asked, nodding towards the bin.

"As long as he stays quiet."

"When we go out, put your head down and keep going. Say nothing to anyone – no matter what they say to you. Just follow me."

She opened the door and strode forward as briskly as the heavy bag would allow. They had to run the gauntlet of a taunting jeering crowd which now numbered about twenty.

"Provo butchers!"

"Keep goin', ye murderin' Fenians!"

"What have you got in the bin, Fox – your father's Semtex?"

"Taigs out! Taigs out!"

They jostled and pushed Rossa as he tried to keep close to his mother.

"Please keep down, James," he prayed.

A fist thumped into his upper arm. He stumbled and struggled to keep the bin upright. The shock of the punch made him whip around angrily to see who had done it. Although the street-light was broken, there was now an ominous glow from behind as the fire took hold. In that glow he could discern the angry jeering faces of the mob. In particular he found himself looking directly into a familiar face. Familiar but now twisted in an ugly sneer of hatred.

Wesley Smyth. He was a couple of years older than Rossa. Lived at the other end of Duncarron Gardens. Wesley had once been his friend. Well, sort of friend. They had exchanged football cards. Wesley had helped him complete his Liverpool collection. "Why don't you follow a real team like Chelsea?" he would taunt. And now?

"Out! Out! Out! Provo bastards out!" Wesley was chanting.

"Come on, Rossa!" His mother marched defiantly through the crowd. He barged ahead with the bin but the image of Wesley's twisted face stayed with him. He didn't dare look back as they eventually forced their way clear of the mob.

The bin was growing heavier with each stride but he knew he must keep going.

"Just another wee bit," his mother panted. "Barney's waiting for us."

At the end of the street a battered yellow van was parked, its engine ticking over noisily. As they approached it, a figure jumped out of the cab, opened the rear doors and hurried towards the couple that staggered wearily forward with their respective burdens. Rossa felt his arms would drop out of their sockets at any moment.

The man took the bag from his mother.

"Hurry!" he whispered. "I don't want that lot after me. Where's the wee fellow?"

"In here," Rossa grunted.

The man paused. "Well, that beats all! Come on! Come on!"

They fell into the back of the van. The doors were slammed shut. Just before the van moved off, Rossa peered through the grimy rear window. The fire had taken a firm hold of the house by now. Rossa felt a sickness in the pit of his stomach. In the distance he could see a land-rover screech to a halt and soldiers leaping out, their gun-holding figures silhouetted against the bright glow. The sound of sirens arguing with each other came to him above the revving of the van's engine. He slumped back against the side of the van.

The lid of the bin rose slowly, mysteriously, then stopped. A tiny voice spoke from within.

"In this day and age," it said.

Chapter Two

In spite of their exhaustion and the terror they had experienced, Rossa and his mother exchanged wan smiles. James was all right.

"I told yis!" the voice snapped from the front of the van. "I told yis to get out of there long ago. Proddy savages. Burning out a defenceless woman and her two children. Savages!" he repeated. "I told yis!" He swung the van violently around a corner. Rossa had to grab the bin to prevent it keeling over. "This is no place for a Catholic family in these times. Especially with no man in the house. Ah come on, ye eejit," he bellowed at the driver in front who slowed down to turn right. Rossa's mother clambered forward to the passenger seat on her hands and knees. "It wasn't always like this, Barney," she said as she sank into the seat.

It wasn't always like this, Rossa thought. It wasn't. There was Wesley Smyth. The face twisted in hatred came back to him. He had lived in Duncarron Gardens for all of his fourteen years. It was a mixed area, maybe slightly more Protestant than Catholic. For most of his childhood that didn't seem to matter – or maybe he was too young to notice. You just played in the street with anybody. Wesley Smyth. Anybody.

Over the past six years things had changed. "Stick to your own kind" seemed to be the watchword. For Rossa the change had been dramatic.

The van slowed down. "Roadblock," Barney explained. "All we bloody needed! Leave this to me." Rossa eased the lid down on the bin.

"Just stay quiet a wee while," he whispered to James. There was no point in trying to coax him out. And there would be no point in trying to explain to the police about James if they discovered him. The van stopped. A torchbeam swept around the interior.

"Name?"

"Barney Maguire."

"Address?"

"Oriel Avenue."

"Is this your van?"

"Every rusty bit of it."

"Your family?"

"No. No, I'm just helping this woman move house."

"Bit late at night to be moving house, isn't it?"

"It's the only time, officer, when you're working all day."

"At what?"

"Deliveries. Coal, gas – that sort of stuff."

"No bombs, I hope?"

"No way. I'd have no truck with that business."

"What's in the bag?"

"Oh that!" He gave the bag a playful punch. "Just clothes. Bed linen. Same in the bin. The big stuff – furniture and that – will be coming tomorrow night."

The officer walked around the van. The torchbeam shone through the grimy rear window. Rossa tried hard to look unconcerned.

"OK. On you go!"

"Right."

"Just one thing." Rossa held his breath. "You need a couple of new tyres."

"I'm seeing a fellow about that at the weekend."

"That's what they all say."

The van moved off again. Its occupants gave a collective sigh of relief.

"Close one," Barney whispered. "If he knew who you were, he'd have us all in for the night."

The bin-lid rose again. "In this day and age," the voice said. Rossa gave a nervous laugh.

"Dead right, young fellow," Barney laughed. "In this day and age indeed!"

James was autistic. He lived in a withdrawn, closed world of his own, refusing to communicate with the outside world. As a baby he had been very difficult, often spending hours in a corner banging spoons off anything that made a resounding noise. Rossa had often lost his temper with him, something which made James even more disruptive and destructive. Rossa remembered one occasion when James littered the kitchen floor with tea, flour, sugar, rice, milk – anything he could lay his hands on. Later he went through a tearing stage – papers, books, wallpaper, clothes. Rossa had got into major trouble in school when he opened his schoolbag one morning to discover every single book and copy in flitters. He had to wait in the principal's office for an hour until his mother came down to explain.

His mother. He glanced at her now, leaning forward in the passenger seat, head in hands. How had she coped with James – and everything else . . . He wondered if that was why his father had left – because of James. His mother would never say.

James had no interest in toys but the one thing he developed an interest in was a terrapin. Wasn't it Wesley Smyth who had one? Yes. Rossa gave a wry smile as he remembered the face full of hate he had seen earlier. He wondered what had attracted James to the terrapin. Was it because the terrapin too lived in a private world under his shell? Whatever it was, the coming of Rocky brought a small measure of peace to the Fox household. And then six months ago when . . . when . . . He stifled the shudder that rippled through his body. Six months ago James had decided to live in the bin. Not all of the time but particularly when he was agitated or upset. Sometimes it was comical. While Ross and his mother watched television, the bin sat in the middle of the floor, lid slightly raised with two little eyes peering through the gap. Or on a particularly difficult day the bin would be parked at the table. The lid popped up, a hand emerged to grab some food, then disappeared as the lid plopped softly back again.

James spoke very little. When he did, it was usually in repetitive one-word utterances (Rocky! Rocky! Rocky!) but of late, for some inexplicable reason, he had latched on to particular phrases which he would repeat at unexpected moments. "In this day and age" was one of these phrases. And now here he was, enclosed in his bin-world, travelling Rossa knew not where in this rickety van. The water in the terrapin tank sloshed about as

10

Barney negotiated the van though a maze of narrow streets. He eventually turned into a redbrick terrace. "Here yis are! The Devlins will look after you." Barney leaped out of the van and knocked on the door of No 14 Oriel Terrace. A slightly-built young woman opened the door.

"There you are, Eileen. The flight into Egypt is here," Barney chuckled.

Eileen Devlin embraced her friend Maureen Fox and guided her into the house. As Rossa lifted the bin out of the back of the van, he could hear his mother's anguished sobs growing in intensity within the house.

Rossa and James were accommodated in a small bedrom at the back of the house. James was offered the only bed while Rossa was prepared to sleep in a sleeping-bag on the floor, but the strange surroundings intimidated James and he insisted on staying in the bin. After much coaxing a compromise was reached. The bin was tipped on its side and the sleeping-bag was stretched into it so that the upper half of James's body was still inside the bin.

Rossa lay back in the bed and reflected on the night's events. It still seemed unreal to him. He half-expected to return home in the morning and see the house intact but the images of the balaclava-clad figures illuminated by petrol bombs reinforced the reality. And above all, the hatred-filled face of Wesley Smyth as he taunted and jostled Rossa when they fled the house . . .

"Out! Out! Out! Provo bastards out!"

The words still rang in his ears.

He switched on the bedside light and reached for the biscuit-tin that lay under his leather jacket. James turned restlessly and mumbled something in his drowsy state. Rossa gently prised the lid off the tin. An assortment of football cards, newspaper cuttings and photographs lay within. On the top lay the most recent cutting. He read it again.

Bomber Gets 20 Years

Provisional IRA bomber Patrick James Fox was yesterday sentenced to 20 years' imprisonment for his part in the bombing of the Manor Inn public house in May of last year. Two people died in the explosion. Fox, aged 38, of Duncarron Gardens, showed no emotion on hearing the sentence but waved defiantly to friends in the court gallery as he was led away from the dock . . .

A photograph accompanied the report. It showed a gaunt long-faced man with thick black shoulder-length hair. Patrick Fox, the caption said. His father. The photograph meant little to Rossa. It was not the father he remembered. He had seen very little of his father over the past five years. He paid infrequent visits, usually late at night. Rossa was often wakened, not by his father's coming, but by the arguments and rows that usually ensued. Once Rossa had stumbled bleary-eyed downstairs to find out what was wrong. His father, surprised by the intrusion, dived behind the sofa while his mother pleaded with Rossa to go back to bed. He lay awake as the arguments continued downstairs. Snatches of bickering reached his ear.

". . . coming in here, putting us all at risk . . ."

". . . entitled to come into my own house . . ."

". . . not fair on the children . . ."

". . . I'm fightin' for their future . . ."

He would be gone next morning and for days afterwards his mother was anxious and tetchy. There were other visitors too. The police had come several times, usually searching the house thoroughly. On one occasion they had lifted the floorboards in Rossa's bedroom.

There was another photograph – of the father he did remember. It was taken on Rossa's First Communion Day. The date was written on the back – 7th May 1968. He stood proudly between his mother and father in the churchyard. His mother held the hand of a shy little girl with blond hair . . . Rossa's hand began to tremble. He slid the photograph underneath the football cards and eased the lid back onto the biscuit-tin. He switched off the bedside light. Please, he prayed, please don't let the nightmare return . . .

The following day crawled by. Rossa felt uncomfortable in the strange house whose small rooms restricted his movement. James spent the morning arranging and re-arranging a collection of shoes he had found under the bed. In the afternoon when his mother went out to make phone-calls, James retreated to the bin from where he watched television. When the early evening news came on Rossa reached to change channels but before he could do so, a familiar scene appeared on the screen. It was Duncarron Gardens. The camera focused on the smouldering shell of a house. His home. Rossa shuddered at the sight of the blackened walls, the gaping window-frames. He was oblivious to the interview that went on in the foreground and stared incredulous at the haunting scene in the background. The camera suddenly zoomed into a close-up of debris scattered in the front garden. It lingered on a charred football boot. Rossa felt himself choking with a mixture of terror and anger. He jumped up and switched off the television. A shrill prolonged scream came from within the bin.

"Shut up! Shut up! Shut up!" Rossa shouted, slamming down the lid of the bin as he stormed out of the room. He raced up the stairs and flung himself on the bed he had slept in, crying tears that would not come.

His mother returned shortly afterwards, much to the relief of a frightened and bewildered Eileen Devlin. She spent a long time calming James down before she confronted Rossa in the bedroom.

"There was no call to do that – especially in someone else's house!"

Rossa did not reply.

"I said there was no – "

"There was every call!" He turned to face his mother. "You didn't see what I saw on telly. Our house is – "

"I did see. I was there." His mother fought to control her emotions. "Now go down at once and apologise to Eileen. You scared the wits out of her."

He didn't move.

"I'm waiting."

Eventually he slid off the bed, went downstairs and muttered an embarrassed apology to Eileen.

"It's all right, love. I understand," Eileen whispered as she put her arms about him. Rossa felt even more embarrassed. His mother said no more until they sat down to tea that evening.

"I've made a decision, Rossa. We're going to Clare."

"Clare who?"

"Not Clare who. County Clare. Where Aunt Rosaleen lives. She can put us up."

"County Clare? But that's hundreds of miles away – "

"Exactly!"

There was a long awkward silence which was eventually broken by the voice from inside the bin.

"In this day and age!" it said.

Chapter Three

"I'm not going!" Rossa burrowed the toe of his shoe into the carpet.

"You are going. We're all going." His mother stared defiantly at him.

"But I don't know anyone there. And it's out in the bog, anyway – "

"And this is better? To be living in fear of bombs and bullets every time you go out the door? And now to be burned out of your own house and be mocked and jeered by your so-called neighbours? I've had enough, Rossa. I've lost enough – " Her voice wavered as she gave her son a look that disquieted him. Her eyes seemed to accuse him – as if she suspected, as if she knew . . .

Rossa could hear glass shattering inside his head.

"Well, what about James? What's he going to make of living – down there?" He stuttered the words as he tried to deflect the attention from himself.

"James'll manage. We'll all manage – with a bit of

16

effort. And don't talk of it being 'down there' – like it was hell. Hell is up here, Rossa, and I for one have had enough of it."

She stood there, eyeballing him, awaiting any further arguments he might put up. He shrugged his shoulders and turned away.

"We leave on Sunday morning," his mother said.

The prospect of a very long journey into a strange part of the country was daunting enough, but when Barney Maguire's yellow van rattled up to the Devlin's doorway on the Sunday morning, Rossa's heart sank.

"Surely we're not going to Clare in *that*?" he exclaimed as he peered through living-room curtains in disbelief.

His mother struggled to get James' arms into his anorak sleeves.

"Well I'm awful sorry. I really am – but all the limousines were booked up for today!" she snapped.

Rossa ignored her sarcasm.

"We'll not get as far as the border in that thing," he mused as he watched the black smoke billow from the van's shuddering exhaust. "Could we not go in the train?"

"We haven't the money to go by train – and even if we did, we'd have problems with this fellow. Wouldn't we, James?"

She brushed the younger boy's hair briskly, much to his dislike. She sharpened her tone again.

"We'll get there with a bit of co-operation all round," she said as she turned to face Rossa with a threatening look. "Now get this lad's bin and for God's sake don't forget Rocky!"

Barney Maguire opened the rear door of the van with some difficulty.

17

"Maguire's Express Taxi! Distance no object!" he chuckled. "Now, gentlemen, move along to the first-class carriage, if you will!" Rossa leaped aboard and waited as Barney hoisted the bin towards him. Together they wedged the bin alongside Barney's addition to the van furnishings – a back seat that had come from a crashed car.

"Now, ses he," Barney panted, "the hostess will be along with the drinks' trolley shortly!" He peered into the bin. "Sure, it's the only way to travel, isn't it, wee fellow? – in this day and age?" he laughed.

Despite his fears about the journey, Rossa found himself being won over by Barney's cheeriness. Maureen Fox embraced her friend Eileen Devlin and clambered into the front passenger seat of the van. Eileen waved in to the boys in the rear.

"God bless ye! Ye'll be grand!" she called as she fought back the tears.

The van took off with a grinding of gears and, as it negotiated the corner at the end of Oriel Terrace, Rossa felt the car seat under him slide across the van-floor. It was going to be an eventful journey.

An hour later, they reached the border. Barney negotiated the van through a security checkpoint. The besmirched face of a young soldier peered in through the driver's window.

"What have we got here, then? Off to the Costa del Sol, are we, Pop?"

"I'm just doing this woman a wee favour. She's making a new start with the kids down south."

"Kids? I only see one – "

"The other's in the bin." Barney decided that honesty would pay off in these circumstances.

"And I'm the grand old Duke of York! Let's have a closer look, then."

The soldier went to the rear of the van and clambered in. He crept cautiously towards the bin and slowly lifted the lid.

"Please don't frighten him," Maureen pleaded. "He's – nervous . . . "

"Well blow me down. I've seen it all now!" the soldier said on seeing the cowering figure curled up in the bottom of the bin. "Is he a bit – ?"

Rossa cut the question short.

"He just likes to be with his terrapin."

The soldier retreated from the rear of the van and came around to Barney again.

"What a strange bloody country! All right, Pop, on you go!" He waved the van through the checkpoint.

"Pop! I'll 'Pop' ye," Barney muttered through gritted teeth, as he drove off. "Young pup, barely out of nappies and he comes over here to order us about! Pop!" He spat through the open window.

They left the Dublin road at Dundalk and chugged their way across the midlands. The countryside was slowly awakening from its winter slumber. The warm late April sunshine was encouraging the first shoots to appear in the hedgerows. From what he could see of the countryside Rossa could discern little change from the little he had seen of the Antrim landscape, except that here it was flatter. No mountains. He remembered going for a drive to the mountains on his first communion day. It was a happy day. His dad had borrowed a friend's car and they had a picnic in the forest – just himself, Dad, Mum, James who was a tiny baby then, and . . . and . . .

He could hear glass shattering again. Change the subject. Think of something else. Quickly.

"Will we be stopping soon?" he asked nervously.

"Aye – we're nearly in Athlone," Barney replied. "The centre of Ireland, they used to tell us at school. We'll stop there and 'Pop' will treat yis all to a bite."

"Here y'are, James!" Rossa slid the burger and chips under the lid of the bin. His brother had refused to leave the bin, let alone the van. A hand came slowly up and took the food from Rossa.

"Do you want to go to the toilet, James? We've a long way to go yet, Barney says."

"Don't want to go to the toilet. Don't want to go to the toilet. Don't want – "

"All right! I only asked!"

Rossa shrugged his shoulders, made an aimless gesture to his mother and Barney through the café window, and went for a stroll down the street. In the short distance he walked, he could sense the difference: the accents of a group of girls, huddling in a shop doorway . . . no boarded-up windows . . . no ramps on the streets . . . no slogans on gable walls . . . and, above all, no soldiers. A sharp squeal of car-brakes made Rossa whip around instinctively and brace himself. A car had shot out from a laneway onto the street almost into the path of an oncoming van. Angry insults were exchanged by the drivers before Sunday afternoon quiet was restored. Rossa smiled and returned to Barney's van.

They resumed the tedious journey. Rossa gradually grew accustomed to the sliding car seat and slipped into a pleasant doze. He was abruptly wakened by anxious cries from the bin.

"Toilet now! Toilet now!"

Barney pulled into a gateway.

"Come on, James," Rossa sighed.

The fading evening light made it difficult for Maureen Fox to read the instructions which had been hastily scribbled on an envelope.

"I took these down in a hurry on the telephone," she muttered. "We should be at a crossroads by now. Maybe we should stop and ask."

"I would – if there was anyone to ask," Barney gave a tired laugh. "Man dear, how do they stand the quiet round here – hold on, there's a crossroads coming up – and a house, with a light! Begob – civilisation at last!"

"It should be a shop." Maureen strained to read the instructions. "Low-ney's, I think."

"The local shopping centre, no doubt!"

Barney slowed the van as they approached the building. A muddy yellow light from a window pierced the gathering gloom. An assortment of cereal boxes were stacked to almost the full height of the window-space. Above the window, through the flaked and peeling paint on a signboard, they could just discern the words Lowney's General Stores.

"Anyone for a Chicken Tandoori?" Barney chuckled.

"We're nearly there now," Maureen said with obvious relief. "Just a mile, Rosaleen says – the seventh house on the left. Count them, Rossa!"

Rossa leaned forward between his mother and Barney. Through the mud-spattered windscreen he could barely make out the silhouettes of the houses they passed.

"Six." He peered out with growing anxiety into the dark landscape.

"Seven! That's it!"

Barney swung the van into a rough potholed driveway. The occupants bounced around as the van lurched crazily towards the house.

"Mother of God! We're back in the trenches," Barney muttered.

The headlights revealed a neat newly-built bungalow. Even before they rumbled to a halt, the front door opened and a woman rushed forward to greet them. She opened the passenger door and paused momentarily.

"Och, I'm sorry. I should have warned you about the driveway. I've been watching out for you for ages. How are you, love?" The tears rolled freely from her eyes as she looked into her sister's tired face. They embraced for a long time. "You're welcome," Rosaleen sobbed. "You're all welcome to Portabeg."

Maureen, Barney and Rossa stepped out of the van.

"My! My!" Rosaleen exclaimed on greeting Rossa. "I wouldn't know this big man. I haven't seen him since – since . . ." Her voice trailed off as she threw an anxious glance towards her sister.

"And where's the wee man?" she asked cheerily.

As if in reply an anxious voice came from the bin.

"Rocky – out! Rocky – out!"

Rossa opened the rear door of the van and carried out the bin.

"Wait till ye see this – it's the best ever," Barney giggled.

Maureen removed the lid and reached into the bin.

"Come on, James, and meet your Aunt Rosaleen."

"Rocky – out! Rocky – out!" James screamed.

"I'll get him," Rossa said. He bent over his brother's crouched figure and groped around the bottom of the bin.

"There he is!" Rossa said, holding the terrapin aloft. "He must have fallen out on the bumpy road."

Maureen eventually persuaded James to climb into her arms.

"Let ye all come in out of the cold," Rosaleen said. "You must be hungry after such a long journey." She led the visitors into the house.

Two girls lay sprawled on a settee watching television.

"Will ye get up out of that, you two lazy lumps and greet your relations!" their mother snapped with some annoyance.

"This is Paula." The elder girl scrambled to her feet. "Paula's fifteen."

"Sixteen next month," the tall girl with the piercing blue eyes corrected her mother.

"And this is Majella." A freckle-faced girl with a roly-poly figure somehow managed to tumble out onto the floor to snorts of derision from her sister. "Majella's thirteen."

"Jelly-baby," Paula giggled. Majella flashed a vicious look at her sister.

"Stop that!" their mother hissed.

"This is your Auntie Maureen from Belfast – and Rossa – and wee James. And Barney's the taxi-man."

The girls nodded shyly towards the visitors.

"Jim's down in the 'mobile' – making sure it's good and cosy for you," Rosaleen explained. "Paula, run down and call your dad."

"Can't. I have no shoes on. Jelly can do it!" Paula replied.

"Really, Paula! Jelly – Majella – will you run down – "

"Why do I always have to do what she won't do?" Majella complained.

"'Cos you're the baby!" Paula teased.

"That's enough! Majella – go!" The girls' mother was clearly embarrassed. "And you, mademoiselle – go out and check that everything is on the table. Now!"

Rosaleen flashed a smile of desperation to her sister.

"Girls! Aren't you lucky you haven't – "

Wrong! Wrong! Change the subject.

"Barney – you'll stay the night? We have a bed."

"Naw! As soon as I get a mug of tea into me I'll be away."

"But Barney," Maureen pleaded, "it's a dreadful long drive."

"No bother!" Barney replied.

There was an awkward silence.

"Actually, to be honest," Barney added, "I wouldn't settle with the quiet around here. Bein' a city man, I'd be a bit afraid of it."

Chapter Four

"God save all here!" The cheery voice of Jim Daly greeted the group seated at the kitchen table. Maureen Fox introduced Rossa and Barney to her brother-in-law.

"And this is James," she motioned towards the bin.

"Oh I've heard all about this man," Jim said patting the lid of the bin. His daughters giggled in the background. "I think it's a great idea living in a bin. I wish I could persuade these two lassies to do it!"

"It's very good of you to take us, Jim," Maureen said.

"No problem. The mobile is in grand condition – sure, we only moved out of it ourselves a few months back when this house was finished. You'll be fine there – for as long as you want."

When they had finished their meal, Rossa and his mother said goodbye to Barney who was anxious to set out for home.

"Are you sure you won't stay the night?" Maureen pleaded.

"Not at all. I'll be grand. You mind yourselves now – and if ever you need me, you know where I am!"

"God bless you, Barney. I can never repay you – for everything." Maureen hugged him, much to his embarrassment.

They waved goodbye as the van bounced along the pot-holed driveway.

The mobile home was warm and comfortable.

"It will take you a while to get used to the smaller rooms," Rosaleen said, "but you have everything you'll want – even the television!" She gestured towards a portable TV in the corner of the long room. "There's a fold-up bed in this room," she added. "I thought Rossa might sleep here."

"We'll be grand – won't we, Rossa?" He knew his mother was struggling to control her emotions.

"Yeah – sure." He was aware of the girls whispering in the background.

"Now we'll clear out of here and give you a chance to settle in," Jim broke in on the silence. "It's like a railway station in here." As he turned to shepherd his daughters out of the crowded room Paula called back to Rossa.

"Will you meet us off the school bus tomorrow at 'Lovely's'?"

"Lovely's? – what's that?"

"The shop up at the cross – Lowney's."

"Why is it called Lovely's?"

"You'll see. Will you meet us? Half-four?"

"OK."

"Jellybaby wants to show you off!"

"I do not! I hate you, Paula – and don't call me Jellybaby!" The younger girl began to thump her sister viciously.

"Out! Out!" their father roared. "Lord give me patience with you two!"

Rosaleen hugged her sister.

"Goodnight, love," she whispered. "If you need anything, we're only a shout away."

The star-filled window above his head intrigued Rossa. He had stood at the window for a long time peering into the night outside. There was so much sky to be seen – and he had never seen so many stars. A myriad of them, stretching to the farthest horizon. It was as if he had moved to a different planet. With aliens for cousins, he mused to himself.

When he eventually slid into bed, sleep would not come. His mind was confused by a succession of images – blazing curtains, faces contorted in anger and hatred. Wesley Smyth chanting "Provo bastards out!", the smouldering shell of his home on the television screen, the long journey across the country in Barney's van. And now the silence. Broken only by the occasional lowing of a cow and the strange and frightening shrieks of a wild animal. Within his new home there was not an absolute silence. In the confined space he could hear mutterings from James and stifled sobs from his mother. Sleep was not coming easily to anyone in the mobile home. Rossa turned away from the starry window and drew the blankets over his head. Please let me sleep, he prayed, and please, please, please – no nightmares . . .

"Good lad yourself!" the old man on the bicycle called out to Rossa. He mumbled a reply. He met no one else on the walk to Lowney's Cross. A terrier yapped fiercely at him until it was summoned by a voice from within one of the houses. What intrigued Rossa were the signs and placards that were erected along the grass margin at intervals of one hundred yards or so. Often crudely painted or ravaged by wind and rain, they all proclaimed variations of the same message:

NO DUMP HERE.

PORTABEG SAYS NO!

NO THANKS! KEEP YOUR RUBBISH!

He paced up and down at Lowney's until the school bus finally arrived. He didn't recognise his cousins initially among the group of ten that alighted noisily from the bus. They were mostly girls, wearing school uniforms of green jumpers and plaid skirts.

"There he is! Hi, Rossa!" The others watched with varying degrees of curiosity as Paula skipped towards her cousin.

"Been waiting long? The old bus goes round half the county before it gets here. And there was major trouble at school. Sister Agatha set up an inquisition over something somebody wrote on a blackboard. 'Ye haven't heard the last of this yet'," Paula mimicked in a squeaky high-pitched voice.

"This is Bridie, Maureen, Jamesy, Margie . . ." she raced through the introductions.

"Hold on!" Rossa laughed, "I couldn't remember – "

"This is our cousin Rossa." Paula ignored his protest. "He's come to live with us – for a while."

Rossa gave an embarrassed wave to the group.

"Where's Majella?" he asked.

There were titters of laughter from the group.

"Rossa's from Belfast," Paula explained to the group as she looked about. "I don't know – where *is* Majella?"

Rossa pretended to ignore her weak attempt at mimicry of his accent.

"I'm here," an angry voice blurted from behind the group. Majella was sitting against the wall of the shop trying to untie her knotted shoelaces.

"Jamesy Larkin took off my shoes in the bus and tied the laces in a big black knot. I hate you, Jamesy Larkin!" She was close to tears.

"Here, I'll give you a hand," Rossa said. He walked over to where his cousin was sitting and bit into the knot, tugging it until it was loose enough to prise a fingernail under one lace.

"There y'are!" He handed the shoes back to Majella, who smiled up at him.

"Thanks, Rossa, I – "

Her words were drowned by the roar of a motorbike which came screaming down the road before swerving towards the group. The rider braked violently and the machine slewed around, its rear wheel skidding into the gravelled area in front of the shop. Some of the group had to leap smartly out of its path. One girl stumbled, her fall causing the contents of her schoolbag to tumble out. Nobody moved to help her as the group's attention turned to the helmeted rider.

Rossa moved instinctively to help the girl by gathering up the scattered books.

"It's all right – I can – manage – " the girl stuttered. She dusted off her uniform. She was of slight build but it was the strange expression in her eyes that caught Rossa's attention. She attempted a weak smile as he handed her the books but the smile could not hide the frightened look in her eyes. Rossa bent to chase after some odd pieces of paper that still fluttered about in the dust. Without thinking and without looking up he spoke.

"That's a crazy way to ride a bike. You could – "

"Who's this bucko?" The rider's gruff voice interrupted him. He had removed his helmet to reveal a square-set head topped by closely-cropped red hair. Rossa wondered how such a head had fitted into the helmet.

Paula broke the silence.

"That's our cousin Rossa – from Belfast. This is JJ – my boyfriend," she added sheepishly.

"From Belfast – is he a Provo?" JJ taunted.

Rossa felt his face flush with both anger and embarrassment. He handed the remainder of the material to the girl. He noticed the name "Margie" on a copybook.

JJ became more riled by Rossa's silence.

"Look, bucko, how I ride my bike is my business. You just mind yours!" He turned to Paula, handing her the helmet. "Are you coming for a scorch?"

"Not too far – we're late already, JJ."

She hitched up her skirt and sat astride the pillion.

"Mind my bag, Jelly – and wait in Lovely's. I won't be long!" she called as she fastened the helmet.

JJ gave a parting scowl at Rossa before revving up his machine and taking off at great speed with Paula clinging tightly to him.

The group began to disperse in twos and threes.

"Come on, Rossa," Majella sighed. "We might as well do as we're told."

The bell above the shop-door jangled noisily to announce their arrival. It took Rossa a few moments to adjust to the dim interior. He had never seen a shop like it. Shelves piled crazily up to the ceiling with no apparent order except that the near end was stacked with food, mainly tins and jars, while shelves at the far end sagged under tins of paint and an assortment of boxes. On the floor to his left sat two opened bags of potatoes, a sack of onions and a box of withered cabbages. The shop counter was laden with sliced pans and cakes, while at the far end lay a large tray of bacon, cooked ham, rashers and sausages, all covered by a clear plastic lid.

A figure emerged from the gloom at the opposite end of the shop. A balding tubby man peered through thick glasses at the visitors. His plumpness was exaggerated by a layer of jumpers – Rossa could discern at least three separate collars. The man rubbed his hands busily.

"Lovely, lovely, lovely." He almost sang the words. "Who have we here?" He pushed the glasses close to his eyes and strained to identify his customers.

"It's just me – Majella – and my cousin Rossa, Mr Lowney."

"Oh lovely, lovely, lovely. Rossa – that's a lovely name. Lovely, lovely – "

"Can I have two packets of crisps, please?"

"Crisps? Right." He bent down beneath the counter and began rooting among boxes.

"Now you know why he's called 'Lovely'," Majella whispered. Rossa nodded.

"Shoop!" the voice muttered from below. A cat shot out from beneath the counter past a startled Rossa and leaped up on the onion sack where it promptly curled itself up.

"Now!" The bald head appeared again. "Lovely, lovely,

lovely!" He tossed two bags of crisps on the counter in front of Majella. She slid a small pile of pennies across in return.

"We have to wait here for my sister, Mr Lowney."

"Oh wait away. Lovely, lovely, lovely." He shuffled away to the far end of the shop which Rossa now realised was a public bar.

Majella tore the bag open and began munching the crisps. She motioned to Rossa to do likewise.

"Thanks!"

"I hate being a younger sister. I hate being walked on. I hate being called Jelly. And I hate Jamesy Larkin!" she mumbled through a mouthful of crisps.

"And JJ?" Rossa asked.

"Ah, he's just a big pig. Works in Gorman's Garage up the road. Thinks he's it when he's on that bike. Paula's stupid to bother with him. If Mammy knew she was riding around on the bike with him she'd have a fit!"

"He's not the friendliest of guys, is he?" Rossa said with a nervous laugh.

"No. He doesn't like anyone crossing him."

"I gathered that!"

As he tore open the crisp-bag, Rossa noticed that he still held a sheet of paper in his hand. He stuffed it quickly into his pocket.

"That girl – who let her bag fall – who is she?" His effort to feign indifference failed to impress Majella.

"Oooh! Interested, are we?"

"Nah!" Rossa gave an unconvincing laugh.

"That's Margie Nelson. 'Moody Marge,' we call her. She's very quiet. A bit odd, if you ask me. She lives just a few houses down from us. Do you fancy her?"

Rossa was saved the embarrassment of a reply by the roar of the motorbike.

"The return of Evel Knievel," Majella sighed. "Come on. We're dead late. Mammy will kill us. And remember – not a word to her about JJ. Bye, Mr Lowney," she called out.

"Oh lovely, lovely, lovely," came the muffled reply from the public bar.

The bike tore away again in a cloud of dust.

"God, ye were long enough!" Majella slung the schoolbag to her sister. "Come on, we'll be murdered." She marched briskly down the road. Paula followed, struggling with her schoolbag.

"Keep your hair on, Jelly," she muttered. "You're always fussing!"

Rossa followed a short distance behind the sisters. On an impulse he withdrew the crumpled sheet of paper from his pocket and stole a glance at it. To his amazement, it contained only one sentence, repeated unevenly down the length of the page.

"I am a good girl. I am a good girl," it read.

Chapter Five

"What's with all the signs?" Rossa enquired.

"Oh that," Paula sighed. "Portabeg's latest tourist attraction. The County Council are going to open a dump here."

"Where?"

"In the bog. Out there. Behind the wood."

She gestured to the long strip of pine trees that ran behind the houses. "There's ructions over it. Meetings and marches and everything. Daddy said he'd never have built the house if he knew about the dump."

"And is it definitely going ahead?"

"Don't know. Portabeg says no, but the Council says yes. Jelly won a prize over it."

"A prize?"

"Tell him, Jelly. Don't be modest!"

"There was a competition organised by the Protest Committee," Majella said. "For the best slogan. Mine won. 'We refuse refuse!' I got twenty pounds."

"That's real clever." Rossa was genuinely impressed.

"Our Jellybaby's not just a pretty face," Paula teased.

Majella swung her schoolbag angrily at her sister. They turned into the gateway of their home.

"Mind the potholes!" Paula warned. "You could be drowned!" She leaped over a large puddle.

"There's a big meeting in the national school next week. You should come down for the crack, Rossa!"

"Yeah," Majella agreed. "Mr Nelson is Chairman of the Protest Committee."

"Mr Nelson?"

"Yeah. Your future father-in-law," Majella chuckled.

"What's this?" Paula looked at her cousin in disbelief. "Are you giving Moody Marge the eye on your very first day in Portabeg?"

"Don't be stupid!" Rossa snapped. He stepped right into a deep puddle. The girls snorted with laughter at his misfortune.

"It's love all right, Jelly. Though, as far as I'm concerned, you're welcome to the two of them – father and daughter."

She sprinted towards the back door.

"We're home," she called out. "It's all Jelly's fault we're late!"

Rossa hobbled after the sisters, feeling the water slosh around in his runner.

"And you're welcome to JJ," he muttered viciously.

He studied the page of writing again later that night. It puzzled him even more. It reminded him of the sort of punishment he had got at primary school.

"Very sloppy work," Mr O'Donnell would say. "'I must take care with my homework' – write it out fifty times."

"Ah sir – that's not fair – "

"A hundred times, Fox. Any questions?"

"No, sir."

Just you try doing homework when your brother is throwing a tantrum, screaming his head off and hurling books at you, he thought.

This wasn't a punishment exercise. It was hastily scribbled across lines and in various directions. And why write "I am a good girl"? As he folded the page and put it into his biscuit-tin, he remembered the frightened look in Margie's eyes . . .

"Come on, James. There's no one around. Come on outside for a wee while."

"Bin! Bin! Bin!" was James' anxious reply.

"Ach, you don't need the bin!" Rossa's patience was wearing thin. His mother had left him in charge while she had gone with Aunt Rosaleen to see about a job. Rossa had spent half an hour trying to coax his brother out to the garden. He tried a new approach.

"Rocky would love to go for a walk in the grass — wouldn't you, Rocky? See, he's nodding his head!"

It worked. James held the terrapin in cupped hands and stepped out into the spring sunshine.

"Now let him go for a walk in the grass," Rossa suggested.

"No! No! No! Rocky lost! Rocky lost!"

"No, he won't get lost. He'll not go far."

James relented and knelt over Rocky, watching his every move intently.

Rossa wandered about the garden, edging towards the roadside while talking all the time to James. Twenty to five. He glanced down the straight stretch of road. They were straggled along its length in small clusters. He hoped his cousins were last, as was usual.

"How's Rocky doing, James?" he called out.

James mumbled a reply. Two girls passed by and waved shyly at Rossa. He waved back. Margie approached on her own, head bowed. She would pass right by in silence if he didn't speak.

"Hello!"

She looked up with a startled expression.

"Hi!" she whispered. She slowed her stride but did not stop.

"I hope I didn't – frighten you!"

"No."

"No motorbikes around today, I hope."

"No."

This was useless, Rossa thought. He thought of mentioning the sheet of paper but decided against it. She had passed by. He turned away in disgust, as he heard his cousins' laughter in the distance.

The voice was subdued but he heard it clearly. She had paused momentarily.

"Thanks – for helping with the books!"

She turned away again.

"You're welcome!" he shouted.

He skipped back down to James.

"You're welcome! You're welcome!" he sang.

James scooped up the terrapin into his hands and stared intently at it.

"You're welcome," he said.

"Well – I got the job!" Maureen Fox's expression beamed with both delight and relief.

"Where?" Rossa kept his eyes fixed on the television set where Tom was in frantic pursuit of Jerry.

"Liscrone House. It's about three miles away but Jim can give me a lift every morning."

"Every morning?" Tom had run straight into a frying-pan.

"Well – five mornings a week. But it's mornings only. General cleaning and light housework. Mrs Costello seems very nice – said she'd leave me home each day."

Jerry had tipped up the ironing-board directly into Tom's path. Splat!

"You might at least say congratulations."

"Congratulations."

His mother slammed the saucepan down on the cooker hob and confronted him, blocking his view of the television.

"Look, Rossa, I know it's not ideal but it's something – a start. I need – we need – money for us to live on. We can't live totally on charity."

"I could get a job – "

"Doing what? – where?" Her voice softened. "I know life isn't easy for you – no more than for any of us, but I didn't draw up the rules, Rossa. I have to take what comes and I was lucky enough to get this."

"Couldn't you take James with you and then I could – ?"

"You know that's not on, Rossa. It's hard enough to get him settled here without unsettling him again. I couldn't get my work done. And it's only mornings. Just give me the chance, Rossa."

She knelt before him and put her arms around him.

"I have to be able to rely on you, Rossa," she whispered.

"OK, OK, OK."

In the background the cartoon music bounced along and a voice said, "That's all, folks!"

Even though he had been in "Lovely's" shop a few times, the jangling bell that announced his entry still startled Rossa. What startled him even more was to discover that the only other customer in the shop was Margie Nelson.

"Hi! – Are you – not at school?" he stammered.

Stupid, stupid question.

"No."

Think of something intelligent to say this time. Think!

"It's nice to get the odd day off – "

Brilliant.

"My Dad's not well – so he needed me at home. Mam's at work," Margie explained.

"Oh." Is that all you can say? "I – hope it's not too serious."

"What?"

"Your Dad – "

"No – just the flu."

Now what?

"Lovely, lovely, lovely." The portly figure emerged from the bar, wrapping a bottle in a sheet of newspaper.

"There we are, child. Mind you don't drop that now. Lovely, lovely, lovely."

He took the money from Margie and began searching in a tray for change.

"Are you – going home now?" Rossa asked tentatively.

"Yeah – but I'm in a – "

"Can you wait – just a few minutes? I have only a few things to get."

Please say yes. Please.

"I can't really – "

"Please?"

"OK, but just – "

"Half-dozen eggs, two tins of beans and twenty Players." Rossa blurted out his order.

"Lovely, lovely, lovely! Beans, beans – "

"They're over there – to your right – no, further," Rossa said. "And twenty Players."

To his dismay, Lovely went off to the bar in search of the cigarettes. Rossa gave an appealing glance towards Margie.

"Sorry about this!"

"Now – lovely, lovely, lovely – "

"And a half dozen eggs." Rossa craned over the counter to see where the eggs were. The bald head disappeared under the counter.

"Lovely eggs! Lovely, lovely, lovely." He emerged holding a plastic basin full of eggs. To Rossa's horror, he began to wrap the six eggs individually in strips of newspaper. Rossa took each one from Lovely as soon as it was wrapped.

"It's OK – I have a bag here. How much is that?"

Lovely picked up a tattered copybook and licked a pencil-stub before slowly jotting down the prices of the three items.

I don't believe this, Rossa thought.

"Is your cash register not working?" he snapped with some sarcasm.

"No. Not since the decimal came in."

He began totting up the total.

"Maybe it might not last, they tell me."

"What?" Rossa cried in desperation.

"The decimal – "

"It comes to a pound and five pence," Rossa said, reading the figures upside down. "Here. Thanks!" He tendered the exact amount.

"Lovely, lovely, lovely. You're a smart lad."

Rossa made for the door.

"Goodbye, Love – Mr Lowney."

"Lovely is something else, isn't he?" Rossa said as they turned down the Portabeg road.

"You get used to him," Margie replied.

"I suppose so."

They strolled on, speaking little, but that didn't matter to Rossa. It was pleasant just to be with someone who didn't taunt or tease.

"What are you smiling at?" Margie asked suddenly.

"It was just thinking about Lovely saying the decimal might not last!"

They passed by one of the protest signs.

"I heard your father is in charge of the protest."

"Mmm."

"Will you win?"

"Don't know. Dad says we must."

"Do you have any brothers or sisters?"

"Why do you ask that?"

The frightened look was back. Shut up, shut up, shut up.

"Just – curious. Sorry."

She quickened her stride.

"No. I'm the only one."

"Bet you're spoiled rot – " She stared angrily at him. Talk about foot-in-mouth disease . . .

"It doesn't always mean – "

"I know. Sorry. That was stupid of me."

"You have a brother."

"Yeah. James. He's autistic."

"What's that?"

"Just lives in his own world. Lives in a bin half the time."

"In a bin?"

"Yeah. That's his world. He can be a right wee divil at times." He recalled James's paper-tearing exploits and the trouble he caused Rossa at school.

"Is that all?"

"What do you mean?"

"Is that all your family?"

It was his turn to be defensive.

"Yes." Go on. Tell her. Tell her. "I had a sister . . . she died."

"Oh – I'm sorry."

A long silence followed. They were approaching Aunt Rosaleen's house.

"I'll see you around, I suppose," Rossa said.

"I suppose."

"I was – thinking of going out to the bog at the weekend. I've never really seen one. Would you like to come?"

"I don't know. I –"

She was interrupted by Maureen Fox's hysterical screaming. Rossa raced through the potholes and burst through the door.

"What is it, Mum? What is it?"

"Oh Rossa. Help me! Help me!" his mother sobbed.

"OK. I'll help you. Just calm down and tell me what's wrong."

She looked at him with terrified eyes.

"It's James. He's gone!"

Chapter Six

"Gone? He couldn't be gone!"

"I'm telling you he is. I've looked all around the garden. I've called him and called him –" Her voice broke into staccato sobs. "There was – no answer – from – anyone. There's – no one – anywhere."

Rossa initially felt embarrassed by his mother's tears and cast an anxious glance at Margie who had followed him inside the mobile home.

"Don't worry, Mrs Fox. He can't have gone too far," Margie said. "We'll find him." She turned to Rossa. "I'll just run home with this," she said, holding up the bottle wrapped in newspaper.

Rossa nodded and, lifted by Margie's support, he spoke reassuringly to his mother.

"Yeah, we'll find him, Mum. The wee rogue – he's probably hiding in someone else's bin!" He made an attempt at laughter but knew it wasn't convincing.

"He – wouldn't – go near – anyone." His mother shook her head repeatedly as she spoke.

Rossa felt a rising sense of panic. He raced to the

bottom of the garden and scrambled up the high bank which separated the garden from the field beyond. He cupped his hands about his mouth and called James's name at the top of his voice. Only a faint echo answered him. He scanned the surrounding fields and back gardens for any sign of movement. Nothing.

He ran back to the road. In the distance he could discern the figures of the students returning from school. Without thinking, he dashed towards them, throwing glances to left and right as he ran. He was breathless by the time he reached the leading group.

"Have you – seen – James – the wee fella?" he panted.

They shook their heads, bemused by Rossa's frantic appearance. Paula and Majella hurried towards him, sensing that something was wrong.

"It's James – he's disappeared," Rossa explained. "Keep an eye out for him – he can't be far away."

He sprinted back to where his mother waited anxiously by the roadside.

"Nothing."

Margie had returned and was waiting for him also.

"Look, Mum, Paula and Majella are on their way. Margie and me'll work our way up through the back gardens of the other houses. He has to be there – probably stuck in a hedge and afraid to move! You stay here – in case he comes back by himself."

They set off, clambering over fences and searching in every outhouse and secluded corner, calling out James's name. They were approached by some residents who initially objected to intruders in their back gardens but relented on hearing why the young people were in distress. Nobody had seen James and, when they reached the last house on the road, Margie could read the desperation in Rossa's face.

"We could try the wood," she suggested. He nodded. The wood was a narrow strip of pine trees that ran behind the houses, separating them from the bogland beyond.

"We can go back to Aunt Rosaleen's that way. Maybe he has turned up in the meantime." He knew his voice lacked conviction.

They spread out to either fringes of the wood – Margie on the houses side, Rossa on the bog side. A rising wind sighed through the pines, which returned their calls with a deepening echo. The dark which seemed to crawl in from the bog was even more pronounced in the wood.

Rossa paused to gaze across the bog. It seemed a forbidding, hostile place to him now. Here and there he caught a glimpse of the dark sheen of a pool. He shuddered. If James had gone that way, there was no knowing . . .

They reached the end of the wood. Margie shrugged her shoulders and attempted a smile.

"We'd better get back, I suppose," Rossa said with a resigned sigh.

A small group of people stood in a huddle on the roadway. Rossa was relieved to recognise Jim and Rosaleen among the group. His mother came to meet him.

"Well?"

"Nothing. No sign of him anywhere."

His mother buried her face in her hands.

Jim Daly approached with the rest of the group.

"Where did you look?"

"We went up through the back gardens," Rossa gestured towards the row of houses, "and came back through the wood."

"And there was no sign of him?"

"No. I just said that," Rossa snapped. Of course there was no sign of him, he thought. What does he think – I have James in my pocket?

"All right, all right." Jim had sensed the tension in Rossa's voice. "What we have to do is remain calm and get organised." He looked at the darkening sky. "We have about an hour of daylight left. I suggest we try the bog."

About twenty searchers had been mustered by the time they set off. They were issued with a description of James and instructions about working together and scanning the bog for anything unusual – a piece of clothing, a tissue, a crisp-bag. There were warnings too.

"The bog is a dangerous place – no matter how well you think you know it," Jim Daly addressed the group. "So stay close together and don't take any chances. We'll search it in strips rather than try to cover the whole place." He gave an anxious glance at the sky, in particular at a bank of heavy rain-clouds that were rolling in from the west. "We'd better move out. Call out if you see anything."

Rossa was soon to discover the truth of Jim's words about the nature of the bogland. It was his first time to experience terrain like this and he quickly found out how deceptive it was. The bracken-covered surface hid a variety of water-channels and little pools into which he constantly slipped. Some of the pools were quite treacherous, sucking his leg under to knee-depth. He threw an embarrassed glance at Margie as he dragged himself clear of one flooded pool. She smiled back.

"Watch your step!" she whispered.

The search proved fruitless. As time wore on, some of the younger members of the group grew restless and began throwing clods of turf at each other. When Majella was hit and cried out in pain, Jim Daly turned on them, enraged.

"If that's all ye came for, clear off – now! This isn't a picnic. There's a boy's life at stake!"

Nobody moved. The young people dared not look up. The search resumed. The words "a boy's life" struck home with Rossa. He looked across the wide expanse of the ever-darkening bogland. They had only searched a fraction of the bog.

"All right!" Jim called out. "That's as much as we can do today. We'll call it off until first light tomorrow."

Rossa was dumbfounded.

"But you can't," he pleaded. "He's out there somewhere. You can't call it off now!"

"I'm sorry, Rossa," Jim replied. "It's too dangerous. It'll be pitch dark here in twenty minutes. We'd end up looking for more than one missing person."

As if to give substance to his reasoning, the first spatters of rain beat down on the huddled group.

Rossa ignored Jim's words. He leaped up on a spongy knoll and called out as loudly as he could:

"James! James! Where are you, James?"

Only a rain-muffled echo replied in seeming mockery to his call. Rossa began to cry. A jagged streak of lightning illuminated the sky. Unbelievably, he was sure he heard the sound of shattering glass. Not here in a bog, hundreds of miles from Belfast. First her and now James. No. It couldn't be true. He called the name again. A hand rested on his shoulder.

"Come on, Rossa," Jim said quietly. "I know how you feel but we've done all we can for now. OK?"

Rossa choked back a sob and nodded.

"Good lad," Jim said.

The group moved off, knotted together now for their own safety. Rossa trailed behind them, looking back whenever he could, half-hoping to hear James or see a light flashing. Something. Anything. Margie said nothing but stayed close to Rossa all the way home.

"Chore! Chore! Forish! Forish!" The woman's call echoed across the bog as she strode purposefully through rush and sedge. Her waist-length hair, swept back from her weather-beaten face by a bandanna, flowed behind her in the rising wind. Ahead of her the leaden sky seemed to tumble headlong down the distant hillside.

She paused to scan the immediate area and listen.

"Forish! Forish! Where is that creature? I'm afraid she may have dropped the *uainín* and there's a big blow coming."

She prodded her stick into the dog who squatted on all fours beside her.

"Come on, Pinkerton! Find her for me. *Forish! Forish!"*

She resumed her search. The dog moved out in a wide arc, weaving low between clumps of rushes, turning, doubling back and surging forward again.

"Forish! Forish!" the woman called.

Suddenly the dog gave an excited yelp and darted away to the left. The woman wheeled about to follow him.

"Gread! Gread!" she called, stumbling across the rutted waterlogged surface. The dog stopped and stood rigid atop a mound of moss.

"Forish! Forish!" The woman was breathless now, her voice reduced to a whisper. She staggered forward to lean on the dog's back and peer into the gully below. Her bright blue eyes danced with delight as she grabbed the dog's coat and tugged it affectionately.

"Grazie, Pinkerton, *grazie!"*

Below her, the missing sheep stood, fearful and immobile in a deep drain. The woman slithered towards the frightened animal, digging her boot hard into the peat and clutching a heather root with one hand.

"Chore! Chore!" she whispered as she inched towards the sheep which was wedged up to her belly in ooze. The woman reached down and took a firm grip of the back of the animal's neck with her free hand.

"Anois!" she sighed, summoning all her strength into one mighty tug. She bit into her lower lip and pulled. There was a strange sucking sound as the animal's body slowly rose clear of the dark water.

"Forish!" the woman croaked as she felt the heather root slowly loosen. The sheep, sensing freedom, dragged her front legs clear of the mire and clambered weakly onto the opposite bank. The woman let go and fell back exhausted. She lay there for a few moments hugging the steep bank before slowly hauling herself up onto the bracken. The dog came to her and licked her face.

"Grazie, Pinkerton," she whispered. When she had recovered she rolled over and sat upright. Across the drain, the sheep staggered about in a daze before shaking herself and trotting over to a little hollow in the heather.

She stood there, head bent into the hollow. The woman watched with growing curiosity. She stood up and hurried to a point where the drain narrowed. She leaped across, followed by the dog, and approached the sheep which was now uttering strange low noises.

She was nuzzling the tiny limp body of a lamb which lay in a crude nest in the heather.

"Ara, *a chréatúirín*," the woman cried as she knelt to pick up the lamb. To her surprise the lamb gave the faintest bleat. The woman whipped off her bandanna and wrapped it around the lamb's body. Her hair fell across her face. She gathered the long tresses with one hand and wrapped them gently around the shivering body of the lamb. The sheep watched her anxiously. The woman understood her anxiety and spoke softly to her.

"We must get your *uainín* home to the *tine.*"

She set off, cradling the lamb in her tresses, but was stopped short by the dog's excited yapping some twenty metres away.

"What is it now, Pinkerton?" she called as she moved forward to investigate. Nothing could have prepared her for what she was to find this time. Wet, bedraggled, his tracksuit muddied and torn, a terrified boy sat cowering under a windbent gorse bush. He shrank away from the approaching figure.

"Well, *go bhfóire Dia orainn!*" the woman said very softly. *"Uainín eile ar strae!"*

The boy hid his face in his hands. The woman bent towards him with some difficulty, careful not to hurt the lamb she cradled in her left arm. Behind her both the dog and sheep looked on, bemused.

"Chore!" She spoke gently. *"Chore! Chore!"*

The boy peeped out at her between his fingers.

"Chore!" She placed her free hand on his head. Slowly he withdrew his hands from his face. She gestured to him to come out from under the bush. He fixed his gaze on the lamb curiously wrapped in a colourful cloth and black ringlets. He crawled out and stood before her, his eyes still indicating wariness.

"Chore! Chore!" She reached out and swept his slender body into her right arm.

"Andiamo! Pinkerton, *andiamo!"*

The daylight was quickly fading and the first drops of rain began to fall when the strange procession moved back across the bog. At its head an excited dog, darting and weaving its way, pausing now and then to give what seemed an encouraging yelp to those that followed. At its tail a bleating sheep hopping surefootedly across the rough terrain. In the middle a strong broadly-built woman strode along with a bundle in either arm. She crooned gently as she bounced along. *"Bimba, bimba, non piangere."* The boy reached across to place a finger on the lamb's head.

Chapter Seven

A large group gathered outside Jim Daly's house as the morning light broke across Portabeg. They circled round a garda car and shuffled about in the raw wind as Sergeant Fogarty spread a map across the bonnet of the car and planned the search with Jim and two other men. Rossa stood on the fringe of the crowd with his mother who gripped the collar of her coat tightly about her. Her pallid face and reddened eyes were evidence of a long night of talking, tears and waiting. Rossa was cheered by the sight of Margie on the opposite side of the circle smiling shyly at him.

What are they doing? he thought. Why can't we get going? As if in reply, the huddle over the map broke up and Sergeant Fogarty called the group to attention as two men held the map aloft.

"Now, ladies and gentlemen, a few words of advice before we set out. We're going to start by concentrating on this area." He pointed to the map. "The important thing is – "

He was interrupted by a series of loud calls from a figure who approached the group on a creaking bicycle.

"Attenti! Attenti!"

The group turned as one to face the approaching cyclist.

"I declare to God! It's Lissy!" somebody shouted. Some of the young people began to snigger at the strange figure labouring towards them on a bicycle that looked as if it were about to fall apart.

"She's started training for the Tour de France!"

The sniggers quickly abated when the onlookers noticed the orange crate affixed to the back carrier of the bicycle. As the woman's body swayed from side to side, a boy's head could be glimpsed at one end of the crate.

"It's James, Mammy! It's James!" Rossa cried as he ran towards the woman, followed closely by his mother.

"Have ye lost something?" the woman called as she dismounted.

"Yeah! This wee rogue! Where have you been?" Rossa replied with a mixture of delight and scolding, as he lifted his brother out of the orange crate. His mother swept James out of Rossa's arms and clutched him fiercely to her, emitting strange sobbing noises while her whole body shuddered with emotion. Rosaleen came to her sister's side.

"Is he all right?" she asked.

"He's grand now," the woman on the bicycle answered, even though the question had not been directed at her. "He was lucky he didn't spend the night on the bog, being the night that was in it."

By now the curious group had encircled the strange-looking woman with the long black tresses tied back from her broad weather-lined face with a colourful bandanna. Sergeant Fogarty stood directly in front of her, his pen poised in his hand, ready to record her story.

"I went out last night looking for one *uainín ar strae* and instead I found two – over near Scroogawn," she added, anticipating the sergeant's question.

"'Twas Pinkerton that found him – my dog."

Again she frustrated the sergeant.

"I took them – the two *uainíns* – back to my house and fed the two of them hot milk. By then it was too dark and wet to find out where this *uainín* belonged."

She turned the rusting, creaking bicycle around and prepared to leave.

Maureen Fox eventually released James from her grasp and looked at him through tear-filled eyes.

"Why did you do that, James? Why did you go away? I told you never – "

"Bin gone," James protested. "Bin gone. Bin gone in car."

"I know what happened," Majella suggested. "He saw someone going off to the bog with a bin in the boot of the car – and thought it was his."

"Brilliant, Jelly. Absolutely brilliant." Paula stood in genuine admiration of her sister's deduction. "I wonder who it was that was dumping rubbish in the bog!"

The sisters' conversation deflected attention from the woman who had now mounted her bicycle and creaked away from the bemused group.

"*Addio!*" she sang.

Instinctively Rossa began to run after her.

"Thanks!" he called out. "Thanks for – "

She waved an arm in acknowledgement and began to sing in a carefree voice.

"Un bel di vedremo
levarsi un fil di fumo . . ."
her voice trailed away.

"Come on," Rosaleen announced. "We'll have a celebration breakfast! You're all welcome!"

Rossa munched a rasher sandwich.

"Who is she anyway?" he asked.

"Who? Lissy? Ah she's a wild woman that lives out in the bog. Thanks, Jelly." Paula snatched two sausages from Majella's plate as her sister passed by, seeking a place to eat in the crowded kitchen. "Lives in a shack with her dogs and cats. I'd be afraid of my life to go near the place."

"She seems to know a few languages. What was she singing?"

"Don't know. She's mad. Loopy Lissy, JJ calls her. Hey, Jelly – any toast?"

Rossa walked to Mass in Liscrone with his cousins on the following morning. He felt conscious of eyes watching him closely in the church yard. He was the stranger, the outsider. Majella and Paula hung around chatting with their pals until the bell summoned them into the church. Rossa scanned the congregation. Please let her be there. Please. There was no sign of her.

Again after Mass, his cousins dallied for what seemed like an hour to him. As he wandered aimlessly around the churchyard, a voice startled him.

"Hey Foxie!"

He turned around to find himself confronting JJ who held a pretend rifle in his hands.

"Now, Provo, put that gun down nice and slow. I'm taking you into custody!" he chuckled.

Rossa blushed with embarrassment. He turned and walked quickly away.

"Come back or I'll shoot, Provo!" JJ bellowed.

Rossa didn't dare look back. Does he know? How could he know?

He was relieved to find that JJ did not follow him. He went into "Lovely's" for a paper. As usual, Lovely was rooting in a tray for change, to the annoyance of a line of customers.

"Hi!" Another voice hailed him. A more welcoming voice. It was Margie.

"Hi. I didn't see you at Mass. Were you there?"

She nodded. "Side aisle. We were late."

"I was looking out. I was thinking of going out to that woman who found James. We never thanked her. Would you like – ?"

"Sorry. My dad needs me – "

"It's OK. I just thought – "

"Would you like a lift home?"

"No, thanks. I'm with Paula and Majella."

"There's plenty of room – "

"It's OK. Thanks anyway."

"See you."

"Yeah, see you."

Stupid, stupid. Why do you always say the wrong thing?

"There y'are now." Lovely handed him his change. "Lovely, lovely, lovely."

After lunch Rossa decided he would try to find the mad woman's house on his own. There can't be many houses out in the middle of the bog, he thought. And it would help pass a Sunday afternoon.

He crossed the field behind the house and entered the wood. He enjoyed the solitude and the shelter of the tall pines. He dribbled a pine cone with his left foot along the carpet of pine needles. *Keegan sells a dummy out to Heighway. Heighway beats his man, cuts inside, shoots. Goal! What a goal!* The pine cone cracked off the bark of a tree some ten yards away. *Liverpool four, Chelsea nil!*

"Hi!" The soft voice startled him. Margie was leaning against a tree, trying to regain her breath.

"Where did you come from?" Rossa dug his toe into the pine needles in embarrassment.

"Visitors arrived – so I escaped! Are you going out to see – ?"

"Yeah. Can you come?"

"Well I'm here."

He forgot his embarrassment. Anyway it was a brilliant goal.

"Do you know the way?"

"I've only been out this way once. You follow the road for – I don't know – a mile or two and it's away in on the right."

They left the wood and took to the winding rutted road.

"How is your Dad?"

"How do you mean?"

"He was sick the other day when – "

"Oh. He's OK now. It was just – a cold he had."

"Paula told me there's a big meeting next week – about the dump."

"Yeah. Wednesday."

"I suppose your dad will be busy with that."

"Yeah. Letters, phonecalls and stuff."

They talked about James, about JJ and about school.

"Don't mind JJ," Margie said. "He likes to show off."

"He's stupid. Thinks that just because you're from Belfast you're a Provo."

"Is your dad still there?"

He had walked himself into that.

"Y-yeah."

"I suppose he couldn't leave his job."

"Yeah." Talk about something else. Quick. "The bog is a funny place, isn't it?"

"I like it. You can get away from people."

"Like JJ," Rossa laughed.

"And school!"

"And Paula and Majella," he sighed.

"And – parents." There was a hesitance in her voice.

"Yeah." He was tempted to ask her about the "I am a good girl" note but she fell silent for a long period. Leave it.

"There it is! Just under Scroogawn."

"Scroogawn?" Rossa queried the strange word.

"It's that hill, beyond the house."

It was little more than a rock mound partly covered with scrub. On top of the mound a solitary tree grew, bent over by the wind.

"There's a story that a saint used to live there long ago, but I don't know."

They followed a rough pathway, so narrow that they had to walk in single file. When the house came into full view, Rossa was taken aback at what he saw.

What had originally been a three-roomed thatched

house was now a two-roomed shambles. The roof at one end had collapsed. The remainder had been crudely covered with galvanised iron sheets. A smoking chimney tottered crazily in the middle of the roof. There was a pane of glass missing from each of the front windows. As they drew nearer, the sound of a soaring tenor voice wafted through the open doorway. Another more threatening sound cut across the music. A black and white sheepdog lay on top of a wall watching the advancing pair. His low growls grew in intensity until he broke into a staccato of angry barks. Rossa and Margie stopped.

"I'm not going to argue with him," Rossa muttered.

The woman appeared in the doorway.

"*Vieni,* Pinkerton," she called. *"Vieni! Vieni! Presto!"*

The dog slunk back grudgingly towards the house. The woman gestured towards the boy and girl.

"Vieni! Vieni!"

They hurried forward.

"Come in! Ye're welcome!"

"Thank you," Rossa said. "We came to thank you for rescuing James."

She shepherded them through the doorway.

"Oh, the little *uainín*. How is he now?"

"He's grand. I'm Rossa, his brother, and this is Margie."

"Margie – *bel nome*!" the woman sang. "Here, sit ye down by the fire. *Scuit! Scuit!*" She swept two cats off a settle bed by the fire.

Margie and Rossa slowly grew accustomed to the dark interior. The low-ceilinged room was totally cluttered. The table in the centre was laden with dishes, pots and an assortment of packets – tea, oatmeal, sugar, flour.

There were buckets all over the floor – some filled with water, others empty. Two sacks of meal stood against one wall. The two cats now curled themselves up on top of the sacks. A dresser stood against another wall, but it was the two pieces of furniture to the right of the dresser that intrigued the visitors.

A beautiful oak-cased gramophone sat on top of a small table. It was obviously the most cared for piece in the whole room. The light from the nearby window played on its graining and on its gleaming hinges and clasps. The record had finished playing. The woman removed it carefully and slipped it into a cardboard sleeve. She bent to open the other piece of furniture – a solid black chest with shining brass fittings. She placed the record in the chest and withdrew another one. As she placed it on the turntable and briskly wound up the gramophone by turning a handle on the side of the machine, she introduced herself.

"My name is Lissy. Not Lizzy as some call me. My father was an Italian gentleman who called me Bellissima – the beautiful one. My mother was descended from an Irish princess of the O'Malley clan. She called me Lissy."

The record began to play. Lissy sang along with the opening bars.

Un bel di vedremo
Levarsi un fil di fumo . . .

"My father was a great man for the opera. He went off one fine day and never came back. He left my mother with me – and his gramophone and records. My mother would sing this song – Madame Butterfly's 'One Fine Day'."

She sang along with the record.

Vedi? Egli é venuto.

You see? He has come.

"But he never came. So here I am with my records – and my family."

"Your family?" Rossa was puzzled.

"You met Pinkerton." She gestured towards the sheepdog, now sprawled on all fours watching the visitors. "'Twas he that found the *uainín*. And there's Butterfly – the beautiful gentle one – Bellissima! She's out in the shed. And poor old Siegfried – the warrior. He's there under the table – he's blind and deaf, but he's been with me for a dozen years and more."

They could discern a sleeping shape stretched under the table.

"And there's these two lassies." She nodded towards the cats. "Violetta – *La Traviata* – the fallen woman. She's the black one. And Carmen – the beautiful gypsy. Figaro is outside somewhere. Figaro – everybody's friend."

"It's quite a family," Rossa laughed.

"Oh there's more – the sheep and the hens – and Tosca."

"Who's that?" Margie asked.

"Look at her out in the paddock. Tosca – *la gelosa* – the jealous one!" As if she had heard Lissy, a goat called from the paddock beyond the yard.

Lissy stoked the fire under a black kettle that hung on a crook.

"You'll have a cup of tea – and some sweet cake?"

"No, thanks – " Rossa began. "We just had – "

"Of course ye will." She rooted among the delph on the table and procured two mugs. She dipped them in a bucket of water and wiped them in her apron. Margie looked apprehensively at Rossa.

"'Tis seldom I have visitors. They all think I'm mad because I sing and talk strange words to my family but I'm just happy. 'Tis the most important thing of all to be happy."

She prised open a battered biscuit tin and took out a madeira cake.

"'Tis only a shop cake, I'm afraid. If I knew ye were coming I'd have made soda bread." She cut three thick slices from the cake. The kettle began to sing. She took an equally black tea-pot from the ashes, rinsed it out with scalding water which she emptied into the ashes and made a pot of tea. She gave Rossa and Margie a mug and a slice of cake each and poured the tea.

"Now. You'll enjoy that!"

"Tienti la tua paura," she sang along with the record. "Keep your fears to yourself," she explained. She broke off a piece of cake and slid it under Siegfried's nose. He lifted his head slowly and gobbled the cake.

Lissy seated herself in a great battered armchair in front of the fire. The record ended. There was silence as they ate and drank, punctuated only by Siegfried's snores.

"Now. Isn't this nice?" Lissy said with a contented sigh.

"Where did you get the names for your – family?" Margie asked.

"From the music." Lissy gestured towards the gramophone. "They're all in the stories. Do you not know the stories?"

"Afraid not," Margie laughed.

"They're wonderful stories. My father sang them all to me." She burst into song again. Her song was interrupted by a repeated faint bleating from the corner opposite Rossa and Margie.

"*O mio piccolo tesoro,*" Lissy cried.

She reached into a cardboard box and withdrew a tiny lamb whose limp body barely spilled over Lissy's splayed hand.

"This is the *uainín* I found along with your brother. She's hardly in it at all, the *créatúirín.*" She reached for a baby's bottle among the clutter on the table and gently nuzzled the teat into the lamb's mouth. It did not respond.

"*Chore! Chore!*" Lissy whispered as she tried again. This time the lamb made a feeble sucking attempt. Rossa and Margie watched, intrigued by the gentleness of the heavy-framed woman towards the tiny creature in her hand.

"Here!" She suddenly thrust the lamb towards Margie. "You try coaxing her! If she won't drink, she won't live. Tell her that!"

Margie nervously took the lamb and cradled it in her arms. It seemed so weak and lifeless that any rough movement would kill it. She nudged the bottle-teat into the lamb's mouth and spoke gently, encouraging it to drink. To her delight, the lamb responded.

"*Bene! Bene!*" Lissy applauded the animal's efforts.

They said goodbye to Lissy, having promised to return.

"And bring the little *uainín* with ye," Lissy called.

"The *uain* – ?" Rossa queried.

"She means James," Margie whispered.

For a long time as they trekked back across the bog, they could hear Lissy's voice echoing across the moorland hollows as she sang along with another record. They spoke very little to each other on the way home. There was no need for words.

That night, James, totally oblivious of his experience in the bog, sat on the floor playing with Rocky as Rossa and his mother watched television.

The nine o'clock news brought them all too familiar scenes of violence in Belfast – petrol-bombing and car-burning.

"We're well away from all that," his mother said but Rossa wasn't listening. He had been distracted by the sounds that came from behind his chair. He turned around to see James looking intently at Rocky and whispering repeatedly the words, *"Chore! Chore!"*

Chapter Eight

The meeting in the hall of Liscrone National School was delayed for nearly an hour to accommodate the unexpectedly large crowd that turned up. To create more space, several rows of chairs in the bottom of the hall were removed. The latecomers would have to stand in that space. Rossa, Paula and Majella were three such latecomers. They wormed their way along the wall to get to the front of the standing section. Rossa had not intended to come to the meeting, initially, but his cousins had persuaded him to accompany them.

"There'll be fireworks," Paula promised him. "The fellow from the Council is coming to explain their case."

"They'll eat him alive," Majella added.

"They will not, Jelly," her sister countered. "We're very civilised around here." She paused. "We'll roast him first," she said, exploding into loud giggles.

On the way to the school, away from their parents' supervision, the sisters quickly shed their reserve.

"God, I'm dying for a drag," Paula sighed. "Have you any smokes on you, Rossa?"

"No – don't smoke."

"Hmph!" She looked anxiously up the road. "No sign of JJ either. Jelly, have you any money on you?"

"I have not – and even if I had, I wouldn't – "

"Yeh, yeh – boring old Jellybaby!"

"Am not boring. Just because you don't smoke doesn't mean you're boring." She quickly tried to deflect attention from herself. "Hey, Rossa, are you looking forward to meeting your father-in-law tonight?"

"Very funny!"

"Oh, you'd better be on your best behaviour," Paula added. "He'll be up there on the stage, watching you!"

Michael Nelson was pacing anxiously up and down the stage, glancing at his watch and then shielding his eyes to peer through the light towards the back of the hall.

"That's him," Majella whispered. "He's watching out for you!"

He was a compact squat figure of a man, balding and neatly dressed in a suit, the jacket of which he kept buttoning and unbuttoning in his anxiety. He gave one final glance at his watch, picked up a clipboard and stepped forward to address the babbling crowd.

"Right, ladies and gentlemen, we'll make a start. Apologies for the delay but, as you can see, we have had a huge turnout – which indicates the high level of interest in this protest about the proposed dump-site at Portabeg."

"Hurl them, Portabeg! Come on the beggars!"

Rossa was startled by the interruption which came from a small barrel-chested man wearing a large cap who stood only a few feet from him. A ripple of nervous laughter ran through the crowd.

"That's 'The Battery' Lynch!" Majella whispered in Rossa's ear. "He's as cracked as fried eggs." The speaker continued.

"As you know, we have made our case to the County Council, in both written appeals and through a delegation which I led last month. Tonight Mr O'Connell from the County Council is here to put their side of the case."

"What case?" a voice roared from the back of the hall.

"Well, the least we can do is give the man a fair hearing, and I hope you will do that," Michael Nelson retorted. He gestured to Mr O'Connell to come forward. The official did so, bearing a huge file of documents which he laid on a chair beside him. He addressed the crowd nervously.

"Good evening, ladies and gentlemen. I think I know now how the Christians felt in the lions' den – "

"Let's see if you are a Christian first!" a voice interjected.

"As you know, this question of a site for a new dump has been under debate now for almost a year. We in the Council have, at all times, been sensitive to the feelings and anxieties of people in this and other localities – "

"Hah!" a disbelieving voice shrieked.

"– but if I may put a few facts before you . . ." He reached into his file for a sheet of paper. "This county produces thirty thousand tons of household waste – and it's growing each year."

"You have a fine heap of it there yourself!" a voice bellowed from the back of the hall, to the crowd's amusement, but Mr O'Connell was in his stride now and he was not going to be deflected.

"The problem is that waste has to be disposed of, and

our present landfill site is nearly full. So we have to find a new site. Not easy! We have examined nearly thirty sites and, for one reason or another, they have failed to meet the required specifications – "

"Too near your own house!" another voice roared.

"Please," the chairman interjected, "let's not get too personal about this."

"We have examined Portabeg," Mr O'Connell continued, "from both geological and environmental points of view, and we conclude that the one-hundred-acre site around Scroogawn would make an ideal landfill area, which would last until well into the next century."

Scroogawn! The word pierced Rossa's memory. Lissy! What would happen Lissy?

"We propose to screen off this area and monitor it regularly – "

"It's still a bloody dump!" a gruff voice objected from the doorway.

"Hear! Hear!" came a chorus of support.

Michael Nelson invited questions and comments from the audience. The comments raised objections on a variety of grounds.

"Scroogawn is an ancient holy place. 'Tis said Laoise, the holy woman, did penance there. You can't surround it with a dump!"

Rossa hoped that someone would mention Lissy. He was too nervous to raise his voice before a strange crowd himself but, to his dismay, no one mentioned the one person who would be directly affected by the dump.

The controversy raged on.

"There's not much point in having tidy towns if all those towns are going to dump their rubbish on our doorstep!"

"Hear! Hear!"

"Is it true?" A seething red-faced woman roared to be heard above the din. "Is it true that another location was agreed on and then overruled because a certain politician felt it was too near his own house?"

The meeting broke into a cacophony of cheers, boos, whistles and banging on the wall-panelling at the rear of the room. The chairman's appeals for order were ignored until the parish priest stood up on his chair in the front row and motioned the crowd to calm down. The din slowly subsided. Mr O'Connell stood up, took a deep breath and said,

"I can quite categorically deny that allegation." He sat down again.

A tall bearded man in a thick woollen jumper stood up and spoke softly.

"Has the Council paid no regard to the damage the dump would do to the flora and fauna of the area? Plants like – "

"Arra, feck the flora and fauna!" a heavily built man bellowed from the doorway. "What we're talking about is the poisoned water, a stink that will knock you flat and rats the size of cats roaming the countryside!"

His interruption effectively ended the meeting. There was a spontaneous roar of approval for his remarks. The roar was succeeded by a deafening prolonged chant – "NO DUMP HERE! NO DUMP HERE!" which continued as the crowd poured out of the hall in disarray.

It took a long time for the crowd to disperse, so high were the feelings running after the chaotic end to the meeting. Rossa scanned the excited crowd anxiously but there was no sign of Margie. An all-too-familiar figure strutted towards him.

"Well Foxie, I hope you have no bombs hidden out in the bog or they'll be buried in the dump!"

The glow from a long pull on a cigarette lit up the sneer on JJ's face.

"Ah leave him alone, JJ, and give me that fag," Paula said, snatching the cigarette. "I thought that meeting would never end, I was dying for this! Crikey!" She suddenly ducked behind Rossa and exhaled with a choking splutter. Her parents' car pulled up a mere ten yards away.

"Do you want a lift?" her mother called.

"No. We're OK. We'll walk," Paula croaked a reply. The car moved off.

"Cripes, that was a close call. Where did I throw that fag?"

"I wouldn't have minded a lift," Majella whined, "I'm cold."

"A good brisk walk home will warm you up, Jelly," her sister said, retrieving the lighted cigarette. "You and Rossa step it out there!" She put her arm in mock concern around her sister's shoulders. "You'll be as warm as toast, Jellybaby – and when you get home you tell the folks that good little Paula stayed back to stack the chairs in the hall – "

"But – "

"Goodbye Jelly, bye Rossa." She was already walking away with JJ.

"You'll be dead safe, Majella," JJ called back. "Anyone gives you trouble – Foxie'll pull his automatic on them!" He gave a wild whoop as the pair melted away into the night.

"Hate her," Majella muttered. "She's so bossy!"

"He's a right pain," Rossa said.

"What does she see in him anyway?"

"He has a bike and a few bob. And let's face it, when you live in Portabeg, there isn't exactly a Robert Redford on every corner!"

Rossa laughed as he struggled to match his cousin's earnest stride. Majella was much easier company on her own. They walked quickly on, occasionally having to leap out of the way of whooping figures who whirred past them on unlighted bicycles. Rossa decided to raise one of the subjects that was bothering him.

"I didn't see Margie there," he said as nonchalantly as he could.

"Woo!" Majella's tone was mocking at first, then serious. "Probably in one of her moods. Or maybe Daddy wouldn't let her go. He can be very strict on her."

Change to subject number two quickly.

"The meeting was right good crack, wasn't it?"

"Yeh. Told you it would be."

"They're going to put the dump at Scroogawn. That's where Lissy lives, isn't it?"

"Yeh." Majella was unconcerned.

"What will happen to her if the dump – ?"

"Hah! Sure Lissy lives in a dump all the time. She wouldn't notice the difference!"

Rossa thrust his hands deep into his pockets and said no more.

The following day seemed to crawl by. James didn't help matters by indulging in one of his passions – setting out things in a particular pattern. Sometimes it was shoes, sometimes cutlery, today it was bottles and jars. He insisted on taking down every bottle and jar from the kitchen shelves – ketchup, sauce, coffee, jam, pickles, vinegar – everything was removed and placed in a particular order on the floor. Rossa decided to let James have his way, hoping there would be no breakages before his mother's return. When he unwittingly removed the jam jar to make a sandwich, James went hysterical.

"All right! All right. Keep your hair on!" Rossa shouted, hastily returning the jam jar to its place in the line. Four o'clock, four thirty. He watched the road constantly. It was nearly five o'clock before he sighted the school group. James decided he would change the order of his line. Rossa slipped out and ambled towards the gateway. Paula and Majella were first. Fortunately for Rossa, they were embroiled in a vicious argument and hardly acknowledged his presence as they swept past.

Margie approached, head bowed, striding purposefully. Rossa suddenly felt strangely nervous.

"Hi!"

She slowed slightly and whispered an inaudible reply.

"Didn't see you last night."

"Couldn't go. Wasn't allowed."

"Oh." She was already moving away and giving him no encouragement to follow. "Why?"

She didn't reply.

He tried desperately to think of something to say. What he did say was intended as a joke, but the moment he said it he regretted it. He remembered the scrap of paper.

"Were you not a good girl?" he laughed nervously.

She stopped as if he had roped her in.

"What?" She whipped around and flashed a look at him. There was terror etched in her face. She turned and raced up the road to her home.

Stupid, stupid, stupid. You great stupid thick! He stormed back into the mobile home and charged through the kitchen, ploughing his way through James's line of bottles and jars. James began to scream, a high pitched sound.

"Ah, put the friggin' things back where they belong, you stupid little whinger!" He slammed the door behind him and threw himself on the settee, pounding the armrest in frustration and anger.

Chapter Nine

The nightmare came back that night. He had been free of it for weeks, but now it returned with more ferocity than ever. The streets were pitch black but the girl on the bicycle was enveloped in a phosphorescent glow as she rode slowly down the road and turned onto the busy street. The cars and pedestrians were dark shadows, barely discernible, moving equally slowly. It was like a slow-motion film. He knew every frame of it. Why couldn't he stop it? He called out to her. She waved back to him without turning or stopping.

She was approaching the shop. He screwed his eyes tightly shut. It made no difference. He could only see her more clearly, in close-up. She was laughing. Maybe if he threw something at the screen . . . He brushed James out of the way and grabbed an armful of bottles and jars. His hands were clammy. His whole body was sweating. He hurled the bottles one after another, but each went through the screen without piercing it. James was screaming and stamping on the kitchen floor. Rossa ignored him. She had dismounted now. No! Don't! Maybe this time she would park the bike somewhere else . . . No! The shop window filled the whole screen. No! Don't! Not there! James grabbed the ketchup jar from him and smashed it on the floor. No! She was pointing to something in the window display. He could see her excited reflection in the heavy glass. No!

The dark became blinding, blinding light. Then the noise ripping open his eardrums. She was sailing magically backwards. A split second before the window exploded, he caught a glimpse of her terror-stricken face. But this time it wasn't her face. It was Margie's. Margie was mouthing the word, "What?" And then the shard of glass – huge, glistening, like a giant dagger. It shot straight at her, straight through . . .

"NO-O-O-O-O!"

For the rest of that night, Rossa sat bolt upright, afraid to go back to sleep. He had been sweating profusely when he woke, but now he was shivering as his pyjamas clung to his clammy skin. He drew a blanket around his shoulders and reached across to switch on the television. As the screen brightened he glanced at his watch. Five past four. The screen was filled with snow. He reflected on the nightmare. Why had Margie come into it just at the end? Just when the glass spear . . . I am a good girl, I am a good girl. Why?

The pattern on the screen changed. It looked like hundreds of tadpoles swimming to the surface, just like the jar in school. School. School was another planet, millions of miles away.

"Stand up, Rossa, and read out your letter," Mr Lennon had said. "Listen to this, boys. This is how a letter should be written."

Rossa cringed with embarrassment. He hated this. Write a letter to the manager of the local supermarket applying for summer work.

A letter. Of course. That's what he would do. Write to Margie. The tadpoles started doing somersaults. Rossa smiled.

"Jar! Jar! Jar!" James screamed.

There was a jar missing from his collection.

"I don't know where it is, James," Rossa pleaded in exasperation. Some hope of writing a letter here, he thought.

"Jar! Jar! Jar!" James persisted.

Rossa searched desperately through the press. "I'm looking, I'm looking."

At the very back of the press he found a musty jar of congealed honey.

"Here it is!" he cried anxiously. Please let it fit. James slid the jar into position. He accepted it. Rossa took up the copybook with relief.

"I'll tell you what, James, if you're very good, I'll bring you up to Lissy later on. You remember Lissy? *Chore! Chore!*"

"*Chore! Chore!*" James parroted his words as he gazed intently at the row of bottles and jars.

Dear Margie,

    This is just a note to say sorry for upsetting you the other day. I didn't mean to do so, but I have a stupid habit of saying the wrong thing at the wrong time. You've noticed? I can explain what I said, if not why I said it – if you'll give me the chance . . . I'm a bit embarrassed to meet you on the road now, so I'll wait until you (hopefully) reply to this.

The meeting was great fun. I even met 'The Battery' Lynch! I was disappointed you weren't there. Do you know that they are planning to put the dump near Scroogawn? I wonder has anyone told Lissy?

Life is as exciting as ever. James is going through his bottles-and-jars game. Every bottle and jar in the place is on the floor and you dare not move or touch one of them. I had to do without jam as a result.

I am going to post this. If I gave it to Majella or Paula, I'd never hear the end of it. I hope you will reply – soon. And I am sorry for what I said.

See you,

Rossa.

PS Did you know that you appeared in a dream of mine last night?

Rossa chewed on the biro top and thought of crossing out the last sentence but he decided to let it stand and sealed the envelope.

"Come on, James. We're going for a walk."

"Chore! Chore!"

"Yeh, we're going to Lissy's later – "

"Chore! Chore!"

"Yeh I know – but I have to go to the post office first – "

"Chore! Chore!"

"And then we'll get some sweets in Lovely's!"

"Lovely! Lovely! Lovely!"

"God, you're as bad as himself!"

It seemed silly to have to post a letter to someone who lived just up the road but Rossa was too embarrassed

to deliver it by hand, and he certainly wasn't going to
subject himself to his cousins' ridicule by asking them to
deliver it. She would have it the next day.

"Come on, James. It'll be dark before we get there at
this rate!"

James was yet again crouched on a clump of heather,
studying it intently before breaking off a sprig to add to
his collection.

"Rocky! Rocky!"

"Yeh, I'm sure that Rocky will love the heather, but
you have enough there to smother him. Come on, will
you?"

James made several more stops before they reached
the narrow track that led to Lissy's house. Once again,
Pinkerton announced their arrival. He lay stretched on all
fours, barking angrily, and looking as if he would spring
at them at any moment. James instinctively clung to
Rossa's jacket and refused to move.

"It's all right, James. He won't touch you – sure you
wouldn't, Pinkerton?" He could detect the doubt in his
own voice. He was relieved to hear a familiar call.

"*Vieni*, Pinkerton! *Presto, vieni!*"

The voice came from the paddock where Lissy was
milking Tosca. The goat became restive as the boys
approached, but Lissy began to sing softly to the animal.

"*Vissi d'arte, vissi d'amore.*"

The music of the milk squirting into the aluminium
can accompanied the plaintive song. The boys stood
motionless at the paddock wall. The song trailed away as
the milk music continued.

"That's your song, isn't it?" Lissy said gently. She
repeated the tune, this time with English words. "Love

and music, these have I lived for, nor harmed a living being . . ." She rose slowly and patted the goat. *"Grazie, Tosca, grazie!"* She cradled the can of milk in her left arm and came to greet the boys. "And how is the little *uainín?*" she asked, placing her hand on little James's head.

"Chore! Chore!" James said.

Lissy laughed heartily.

"He keeps saying that, ever since you found him in the bog," Rossa explained. "What does it mean?"

"It doesn't mean anything. It's just a way of talking to the beasts and the birds. 'Twas a word my mother used. And her mother before her. Sometimes I think it's just that the animals are easier talked to!"

She entered the broken-down cottage and motioned the boys to follow her. A muffled tired bark from under the table greet them.

"Ciao, Siegfried, we have visitors for you!"

Rossa showed James where the old dog lay. "Does he not move at all?" he asked.

"Only when he has to," Lissy replied as she poured some goat's milk into a bottle and added water from a bucket. She fixed a teat to the bottle and bent to lift the tiny bundle from the box by the fire.

"Now, *mio piccolo tesoro,* a dropeen of the goat's milk will do your little chest a power of good." She gently nuzzled the teat into the lamb's mouth. *"Tóg é. Tóg é. Chore, chore,"* she said gently.

James watched intently.

"Here, James," Lissy said. "You hold the uainín!"

She held the tiny lamb forward. James looked confused and nervous.

"*Tóg é! Tóg é,*" she whispered.

James held his hands out and Lissy eased the lamb into the boy's hands. Rossa was fascinated at the power she seemed to hold over his brother.

"You're the second lot of visitors I've had here today," Lissy said.

"Oh."

"There was a gang of fellows jumping about the bog in their big boots and anoraks with some kind of measuring poles. They were shouting out numbers and writing them down in books. They looked very important, or so they thought. Pinkerton didn't like them, did you?" The dog wagged his tail in response.

"Did they not talk to you?" Rossa asked.

"Not at all. Too busy. Do you know who they might be?"

Of course he knew. It must be to do with the dump, but should he tell her? Lissy took the bottle away from the little lamb but let James continue to hold the animal.

"Where were they measuring?"

"Just up the bog." She gestured with her hand. "There was one fellow climbed up Scroogawn. What were they up to at all? Maybe they are going to build a big hotel or something!" She laughed loudly at the thought. Rossa took a deep breath.

"There's talk of opening a dump – "

"A dump, is it?"

"Yeh. There was a big meeting in Liscrone – "

"A dump? Well, *go bhfóire Dia orainn!* A dump?"

"Everyone around here is against it. They say they won't let – "

"Is it that they want to fill the bog with all their

rubbish?" For the first time since he had met her, Rossa detected a sadness in Lissy's voice.

"They won't be let" he blurted out defiantly.

"Laoise won't let them," Lissy said, looking out the door at the rocky mound beyond. "She was the holy woman who lived up there on Scroogawn. Leaba Laoise is on the top of it. Laoise's bed. 'Tis said she would lie up there in all weathers to do penance. She'll put a curse on that lot, surely. A dump indeed!"

A black cat jumped up on the dresser and padded towards the can of milk.

"*Scuit*, Violetta, *scuit!*" Lissy pressed a lid firmly on the can. She moved to the black chest and searched through the cardboard sleeves. She withdrew a record and studied it closely before putting it on the gramophone. "This is Pinkerton's farewell to Butterfly's home," she explained as she wound the gramophone. She lifted the arm of the gramophone and dropped it gently on the record.

"*Addio, fiorito asil . . .*" the voice sang. Lissy sang along with the record in English. "Farewell, flowery refuge . . ." She busied herself about the kitchen, her voice halting as she attempted to keep pace with the voice on the record. "I cannot bear the sad appearance of this place – "

Rossa had difficulty in persuading James to part with the lamb and leave Lissy's house. On the way back, James stopped frequently to turn and wave to Lissy who stood for a long time, silhouetted against Scroogawn. Rossa resolved to help her. They couldn't build a dump beside her. They couldn't. He would talk to Uncle Jim that very evening.

Chapter Ten

"Don't you see, Uncle Jim? They can't put a dump at Scroogawn. Lissy lives there! They can't!"

"Well it's an argument against it, anyway. That's if they are going to site it at Lissy's."

"They are! Lissy said that there were fellows around the place measuring with poles and things."

"I'll have a chat with Michael Nelson about it," Jim said. "It's amazing no one thought of Lissy before."

"No one ever thinks of Lissy. That's the problem," Rossa replied.

When Jim had left the room, Paula and Majella circled around Rossa.

"Now's your chance, Rossa," Paula whispered.

"For what?"

"You can go with Dad up to Nelson's and check out your in-laws!"

"Very funny."

"And meet moody Marge," Majella added.

"She's in a total sulk these days. Did you two fall out or something?"

"No we didn't!" Rossa snapped. "There is nothing to fall out over – "

"Well she's in a dangerous mood," Paula said. "She'd cut you in two with a look! JJ asked her was the end of the world coming and she – "

Rossa jumped and sent the chair skidding across the floor.

"JJ! JJ!" he roared. "I'm sick of you and JJ. The end of the world will be coming if he's not careful!" He raced out of the house.

"Ooh, Jelly," Paula whispered, visibly shaken by Rossa's outburst. "It must be love all right."

The mobile home shook as Rossa slammed the door behind him.

"For God's sake, Rossa, there's no need to take the door off the hinges," his mother called out. He ignored the remark.

"When are we going back?" he asked.

"Back where?"

"Back to Belfast. Back home."

"I'm not sure that we are going – "

"Well I am. I've had enough of this kip."

"Rossa!"

"It's true. People always sneering at you. Passing smart remarks – "

"Like who?"

"Yon pair over there." He gestured towards the house.

"Ah Rossa, they're only having a bit of fun."

"Well it's not my idea of fun. I'm fed up of them. Always going on at me. Pair of sneering biddies – "

His mother slammed a saucepan down on the cooker.

"Look Rossa! Those sneering biddies, as you call them,

are my sister's daughters. We are here at their invitation. As of now, this is our home. We have no other home. So don't talk of going home to Belfast. Do I have to remind you that we were burned out in Belfast? Belfast means nothing to me except pain and loss. Nothing!"

She gave him that look that always unsettled him. Knowing. Accusing. There was a frozen silence before both of them simultaneously moved, she back to the cooker, he to the refuge of the television set.

The next two days were bleak for Rossa. He stayed indoors, not just because of the mist and drizzle that hung depressingly outside. Until he heard from Margie, he didn't want the embarrassment of meeting her. He certainly didn't want to endure the ongoing taunts of his cousins, and the roar of JJ's motorbike speeding past convinced him that staying indoors was best, even if he had to contend with James's hysteria when Rocky disappeared for a whole morning. Rossa spent the morning on his hands and knees searching every nook and cranny in the mobile home for the terrapin. It was only when he had convinced James to stay absolutely still and listen that they found Rocky. The faint scratching sound led them to the bathroom where they found the terrapin behind the toilet bowl.

"Chore! Chore! Chore!" James whispered as he carried Rocky away.

Rossa slumped onto the settee with relief. A faint whirring overhead caught his attention. A fly had become entrapped in a spider's web above the light over his head. Rossa watched intently. The spider appeared from a crack in the ceiling panelling and was poised to scurry down the web. Instantly Rossa jumped up, perched on the arm of the settee and reached up to destroy the web. The spider retreated and, after much whirring and struggling, the fly disentangled itself and made its escape. Rossa wiped the remains of the web from his fingers with some satisfaction. He had no great liking for flies but he knew all about webs.

A knock at the door startled him. He opened the door cautiously.

"How are you?" A cheery-faced postman handed him a letter. "Couldn't find a letter-box. That's yourself, I take it?" He nodded towards the letter.

Rossa's heart quickened when he looked at the envelope addressed to him in neat handwriting. "Y-yes. That's me! Thanks!"

"Good man! Good man!"

Rossa closed the door as he tore open the envelope. Yes. Yes. It was from her.

Dear Rossa,

Thank you for your letter. I'm sorry too. I can explain some things if you meet me at the old school at Bawnmore. You go on past our house for about a mile to the crossroads. Turn left and it's just a little bit up that road. Saturday at about two o'clock. I hope that you can make it.

Margie.

The school was easy enough to find. When he reached it, Rossa reckoned that he could get back home across the fields in about half the time. Mr Doherty used to set problems like that in maths class. Something to do with a right-angled triangle. Wally Parker made them all laugh one morning when he said "The square on the hippopotamus . . ."

Getting away from his own house was the hard part, or rather, getting past his cousins' house. He tricked aimlessly around the garden with a football until he heard voices raised in argument.

"It's Jellybaby's turn. I did it last week."

"You did not. You were supposed to, but you asked me to swop because . . ."

"Watch it, Jelly!"

"It's not fair. She always gets her way."

"Ah poor Baby!"

Rossa smiled to himself. This was his opportunity. The argument was still raging as he darted down the potholed driveway and out of sight behind the beech hedge.

The school was a drab grey shell of a building. One end of it was used to store hay which bulged out through the window frame. Rossa circled the building cautiously until a familiar voice called timidly from within.

"Hi. In here."

He felt awkward, embarrassed about meeting Margie again, remembering how he had upset her the last time they had spoken.

"It's a right queer place to – "

"It's handy and not many people pass this way."

"Yeh, yeh!" He shuffled his feet nervously. "I'm sorry about – "

"I wasn't allowed to go to that meeting."

"Hope it wasn't my fault!"

Margie turned away to the doorway and looked across the fields.

"It was actually," she whispered.

"What?" Rossa leaned back against the hay, stunned by her remark.

"Daddy found out that I had gone to Lissy's with you. Said that I wasn't to be hanging around with you – "

"Hanging about with me? What am I? Something from Mars?"

"He knows about your dad."

"What do you mean?"

"That he is in jail – for planting bombs."

"So?"

"So nothing. He just knows."

"So that makes me untouchable. 'Stay away from him. He's dangerous'."

"I'm here, amn't I? It's just not easy. That's all I'm saying."

Rossa found himself twisting handfuls of hay into crude rope.

Margie moved out to the school yard, now rutted and weed-filled.

"I'll go, so."

"No! Don't go. I'm sorry. I'm not angry with you. It's just not fair that people think – I'm the same as my father."

"Do you want to tell me about him?"

Rossa shrugged his shoulders.

"There isn't that much to tell. I saw very little of him in the past five years. He was seldom at home. When he did come, there was always a row. My mum didn't like what – what he was doing. Then he was arrested for a pub bombing. He got twenty years."

"When was that?"

"Last January."

"And what did you think – of what he was doing?"

Rossa twisted the ropes viciously around his wrists. She was looking directly at him now.

"I don't know. I hate all the killing. He was sort of – two people to me. I remember nice things from when I was little. Playing football with him. He built a swing in the back garden. I fell off it one day and split my forehead – still have the scar!" He swept back his fringe to reveal a two-inch indentation.

"I remember him picking me up – I was only about four at the time – and running all the way to the doctors. He kept saying, 'Sacred Heart of Jesus, Sacred Heart of Jesus!' I think he thought I was dead!"

Suddenly it seemed a lot easier to talk. He wanted to talk.

"There were picnics. First Communion. I remember that. We all went to a hotel. I remember spilling icecream down the front of my new suit. Mammy was furious but he just laughed and laughed. Then he lost his job – he worked in the shipyard. And then all the trouble started. He began disappearing. He just – went out of my life. He was there – and then he wasn't. Then he was arrested for the bombing. His picture was in the paper. But I didn't recognise him. Things got really bad and then last month they burned us out."

"Who?"

"I don't know. Just a mob who called us Provos. There were fellows there that I used to play with. That's when Mum decided that she had had enough and came down here."

"What do you think of this part of the world?" Margie gave a nervous laugh.

"It's hard to fit in. Everything's different. I don't know. Maybe I do seem like a Martian to – "

"Not to me." She turned quickly away to hide her blushes.

"Thanks." Rossa unwound the hay rope. He felt a warmth surge through his body.

"You said that there was a girl – your sister – who died."

"Did I?" The rope grew taut again.

"It's OK if you don't want to – "

"No. I'd rather tell." Don't stop now. Tell her. Tell her. Tell her. "Her name was Sophie. It was two years ago. She was ten. She went down to the shops one Saturday. And then – " He fought to control his voice. "The bomb. The shop window blew out. Right into her face. A big spear of glass went right through her."

He bit savagely into his lower lip. His wrists were manacled once again.

"I'm sorry!" Margie couldn't hold back the tears. "I'm awfully sorry." She walked shyly towards him and reached to let her hand rest on his white knuckles. "I'm awfully sorry. I shouldn't have asked."

Rossa shook his head furiously.

"Yes you should. That's not all of the story."

"What do you mean?" Her hand tightened on his locked hands. She could sense his breathing become more and more rapid.

"She shouldn't have been there. Mum had warned her. She was at work. But I was dying to get *Shoot* magazine. There was a big Liverpool poster in it and I thought they'd all be gone. I couldn't leave James, so I bribed her to go down – gave her money for sweets. It was only down the road. She'd be there and back on the bike in three minutes. And then the bomb. Don't you see? I killed her. I BLOODY KILLED HER!"

"No you didn't! How could you know?"

"She shouldn't have gone. I sent her. I killed her. And then – and then – I made it worse. I told mum that she slipped out without telling me. But she knows. I know she knows. She knows I killed Sophie. I bloody bloody bloody killed my sister."

The rope snapped. Rossa rammed his head into his released hands.

They sat side by side, silent for a long time. In the distance, the shouts of participants in a football match echoed across the fields. They both reacted anxiously to the approaching roar of a motorbike. The machine seemed to slow down as it neared the schoolhouse but, to their relief, it sped away again.

Eventually Rossa stood up and stretched his cramped limbs.

"Well there you are. That's the full story of Rossa Fox, Martian, Provo – and sister killer."

"Shut up!"

"Sorry?"

"I said shut up. You're none of those things. I know it – and you know it too." There was a sharp tone in her voice that he had not discerned before.

He shrugged his shoulders and decided to change the subject. He told her about his visit to Lissy and about the men with the measuring poles.

"I told Uncle Jim. He said he'd see your father about it."

"He has a meeting with the County Council this week.

I think they're going to announce their decision about the dump. Dad was on the phone all week about it."

"He's great to get involved like that – "

"He enjoys it. He – likes to be in charge of things."

She plucked a blade of hay and began to weave it gently into a geometrical shape.

"How is Lissy – and the *uainín?*" she asked.

"The *uainín?*"

"The little lamb."

"Oh, he's hanging on. James was mad about him. Will you be going over to see him again – on your own?

"Why? Do you not want to come?"

"I thought – "

"Daddy goes to Dublin for a few days every month. He's an accountant. Has to report to head office."

They exchanged smiles.

"I'll let you know when. I'd better go now or I'll be missed. If you wait a while – "

"I can cut across the fields to the wood. I'll not be seen."

"OK. See you then."

"See you."

"And remember – you're not – "

"What?"

"Any of those things."

"Thanks."

She gave a little wave and took a cautious look in either direction before hurrying on down the road.

Rossa waited for a few minutes before scurrying along in the shelter of the hedgerows that were already displaying the first green shoots of spring. A raw wind bit into his face but he felt warm.

Chapter Eleven

Father O'Mahony droned his way through the Sunday sermon.

"Only by denying ourselves can we triumph over ourselves . . ."

Paula nudged Majella who retaliated with a vicious elbow jab. Paula bounced against Rossa who only saved himself from tumbling into the aisle by grabbing the seat in front of him. In that seat, Jim Daly whipped around, glowered at his daughters and pointed a threatening finger at them.

"Parents have a duty to encourage their children to practise self-denial and, of course, the best way to do this is by their own example . . ."

Rossa caught a glimpse of Margie in the side aisle. He hoped they would meet in Lovely's after Mass. A shrill voice piped suddenly behind him.

"Ark of the Covenant, pray for us." A tiny woman, dressed in black, was bent in two over her rosary beads.

Paula pinched her nose to stifle a giggle. Jim Daly was about to turn around once more when Father O'Mahony's change of tone deflected his attention.

"There are two notices. There will be a meeting in the national school on Wednesday night at eight to consider the latest moves regarding the proposed dump. All are welcome, although I would hope there will not be a repeat of the distasteful scenes we witnessed at the last meeting. That kind of conduct does not reflect well on our parish.

"The second notice concerns an attempt to start a youths' soccer team in the parish. All those interested should attend at Brennan's Field at two o'clock next Saturday. I think it most regrettable that a foreign game like this should make inroads into the county which gave birth to Michael Cusack, one of the founders of the Gaelic Athletic Association. I think we should support our own culture, but then I suppose I am but a voice crying in the wilderness. Please pass the baskets along for the collection . . ."

Lovely Lowney was more than usually harassed by the after-Mass custom.

"Did ye all rob the bank or something? Fivers, tenners and now a twenty-pound note. Where am I going to get change for all of this?"

"They say you have a pot of money under the bed, Lovely," a voice teased from the middle of a press of bodies at the counter.

"Make sure it's the right pot you pull out," another voice sniggered from the back of the crowd.

"Oh lovely talk all right, in front of the children. Lovely, lovely, lovely. I tell you, I never had this trouble with the old money. Here, take six lollipops and that'll make it two pounds even."

"I don't want lollipops, thank you. I'll wait for my change," Beeny Flynn replied, gripping the counter firmly with one gloved hand while thrusting the other towards Lovely in anticipation.

"Ah, here." Lovely threw a number of coins into the gloved hand. "I'm losing money here. Ye'll put me out of business," he whined, mopping his sweating brow with the frayed cuff of his jumper.

"Hmph!" Beeny Flynn turned to fight her way through the throng. "That'll be the day!"

"Oh, lovely, lovely, lovely, indeed."

Rossa stood at the back of the shop and enjoyed the banter as he waited. He was in no hurry. He glanced anxiously towards the door each time it squeaked open. JJ thrust his head in once and looked around. Rossa dodged behind a burly man who was searching his pockets for change in answer to Lovely's appeal. To his relief, JJ did not enter the shop. To his further relief, Margie did enter some minutes later. He beckoned towards her.

"Poor old Lovely is having a hard time," he explained. "Nobody has any change!"

"Oh God, he'll murder me," Margie sighed. "Daddy gave me a five-pound note!"

"You'd better wait, so." He hesitated, then asked the obvious question. "Will you be at the meeting on Wed – ?"

"What do you think?" she replied with a shrug of her shoulders. "But – "

"Yes?"

"Daddy has to go to Dublin after the meeting – for two days."

"Oh good, I mean, does that mean – ?"

"I'd like to visit Lissy again." She gave a rare smile.

"Sure. We could go on Thursday evening."

She always seemed to read his mind.

"About five? I'll meet you in the wood. Now I'd better get the papers or he'll be looking for me."

"Right. Did you hear about starting the soccer team?"

"Yeh. Are you interested?"

"I might be. I was a goalkeeper in the school team at home."

"At home? Oh, you mean – "

"Belfast." It sounded odd to him when he explained. Belfast – home – no home. "I might go down and give it a try."

"Good luck! I really have to go now.

"OK."

Margie began to move away.

"By the way – " Rossa blurted. She turned to face him. "It's nice when you smile." He could feel the blush creep over his face.

She shrugged her shoulders again and turned quickly away.

"Hey Rossa!" Paula called in a loud whisper, beckoning him towards her bedroom window.

"What's up?"

"Will you do us a favour?"

"Depends. What's all the whispering about?"

"Daddy has grounded the two of us for carrying on at Mass. 'Twas all Jellybaby's fault – "

"Was not, pig!" a tearful voice came from further within the room.

"Ah go back to your sums, cry-baby!" Paula snapped.

"Listen, Rossa." Her voice softened. "I was supposed to meet JJ at Lovely's at three."

"So?"

"So I obviously can't now. So would you ever go up and explain – "

"You must be joking!"

"Ah Rossa – just for me, your poor imprisoned cousin?"

"He hates my guts!"

"This'll be a chance for you to get to know each other better."

"You can't be serious!"

"She's just afraid Bridie Doyle will wipe her eye," Majella muttered from within.

"Jelly, keep your trap shut or else. Please, Rossa?"

"Ach, I don't know. I'll – I'll see . . ."

Rossa approached Lowney's Cross with a heavy heart. He was angry with himself. Why do I let people walk on me? he thought. Why don't I tell Paula I arrived late and JJ had already gone? He turned the corner and almost fell across JJ's bike. There was no sign of its owner. He felt uneasy now. He waited a few minutes, thought of leaving, but finally decided to look inside Lowney's.

"Hey Foxie! Are you looking for me?" JJ was licking a huge wafer ice cream.

"I might be."

"So. What's the story? Are the Provos coming to get me?"

Rossa bristled at the mention of that word. Why can't he just be normal for once?

"God, I'm shaking in me boots, lads. Look!" He turned to a couple of shadowy figures behind him, then took a long lick at the ice cream. "Do you know what you can tell them, Foxie? Tell them I'd lick the lot of them easier than I'd lick this!" He held the icecream aloft, to sniggers from behind him. "And tell them not to be sending a boy on a man's errand!"

Rossa felt a flush of anger rise within him.

"I just came to tell you – "

"Oooh, here it comes, lads. Brace yourselves!"

"– that Paula says she won't be down." He felt a sudden surge of confidence. "She says she couldn't be bothered!"

He turned and slammed the door behind him. His last image of JJ was of an open-mouthed stare with both lips covered in ice cream.

He broke into a half-run and hurried down a grassy path towards the refuge of the wood. Within a minute he could hear furious efforts to start a motorbike, accompanied by loud swearing from its owner. Rossa smiled to himself as he fingered a spark plug in his pocket. He had learned a lesson or two in motor mechanics from Barney Maguire. He took the plug from his pocket, tossed it in the air and, as it fell, he swung his lethal left foot and cracked the ball between the posts. Heighway scores again. Wonder goal!

The atmosphere in Jim Daly's car was distinctly frosty. Jim had reluctantly agreed to let his daughters accompany him to the protest meeting. He barely spoke to them on the journey. Rossa sat uneasily beside his uncle. He could feel Paula's eyes pierce the back of his head like a pair of red hot pokers. She had stormed into the mobile home on her return from school.

"What did you tell JJ?" she demanded.

"What you told me – that you wouldn't be down to see him."

"He says you said I couldn't be bothered coming down."

"Did I say that? It must have slipped out – "

"Slipped out my Granny! You're a right sleeveen, Rossa Fox. And you tampered with JJ's bike – "

"Me? What would I know about bikes?"

"You're just too smart for your boots – "

"Keep your hair on, Paula," Majella interrupted. "Sure JJ got his bike going again. Wasn't he able to bring Bridie Doyle to Ennis last night?"

Paula turned viciously to her sister but at that moment Rossa's mother entered the room. Paula rushed past her and marched back to her own house.

Majella winked at her cousin.

"Nice one, Rossa," she said.

"What was that all about?" his mother asked.

"Ach, just jealousy stuff."

For the second time in a couple of weeks, Liscrone National School was packed with a noisy crowd. Rossa perched on a windowsill and scanned the crowd, hoping that maybe Margie might surprise him and turn up. No sign. No sign either of JJ. He could relax.

Michael Nelson stepped up on the platform and raised his arms aloft in an appeal for quiet. The hubbub died away.

"Good evening, ladies and gentlemen, and thank you for your attendance. I'll come straight to the business of the evening." He withdrew an envelope from the inside pocket of his jacket and took out a letter.

"This letter arrived this morning. It's from Mr O'Connell who addressed our last meeting. It reads:

'Dear Mr Nelson,

Further to our meeting in Liscrone on April 10th and subsequent correspondence, I am to inform you that, having taken all the submissions into account, and having assessed the potential and capability of the four landfill sites, it has been decided to proceed with the site at Scroogawn and Moneenduff in the townland of Porta –'"

A concerted roar of protest swelled up from the floor. Prolonged booing followed as Michael Nelson appealed for order. It was several minutes before he could make himself heard above the din.

"Everyone will get a chance to make his point, if we are patient. If I might be permitted to finish the letter, '– Scroogawn and Moneenduff in the townland of Portabeg – '"

"Come on the beggars! Hurl them, Portabeg!" The Battery Lynch's interruption brought nervous laughter from the audience and a series of raucous whoops from the back of the hall. Michael Nelson scowled in the direction of "The Battery" and continued.

"'We wish to assure you that this decision has only been reached after the most painstaking and exhaustive research. Please be assured also that the most up-to-date technology will be employed in making this landfill secure and free of all hazard to the neighbouring communities. A strict monitoring system will be implemented and an extensive tree-planting programme to screen the site will be initiated shortly. It is proposed to start clearance of the site within the next few weeks.

"I trust the Portabeg community will accept this decision in good faith as the best possible option we have in providing a refuse disposal service which will, of course, be of benefit to them as well as to the people of East Clare.'"

Uproar ensued again and when eventually it abated, a succession of speakers voiced their opposition. Rossa recognised a red-faced woman whose allegation of political interference had caused mayhem at the previous meeting.

"I moved here so that I'd have a quiet, peaceful and healthy place to bring up my kids. I didn't move here to live with pollution, stink, rats and ten-ton trucks rumbling past my door every hour of the day!"

The hall echoed with cheers of approval.

"Let's be clear about this," she continued. "This is war on Portabeg. And if it's war they want, it's war they'll bloody get."

Her words set the tone for the remainder of the meeting. There were threats of sit-down protests, calls for action from TDs, a proposal to ensure television coverage of Portabeg's opposition to the dump. Jim Daly finally made it to the platform.

"There's one person who is directly involved in all of this and no one has mentioned her yet. It's Lissy. I know a lot of you think she's a bit – "

"Loopy!" a voice called from the doorway.

"If you like, but she could be our trump card here. She lives right beside the dump-site – "

"She lives in a dump-site!" the voice from the doorway guffawed to ripples of laughter.

"Ah come on, fair is fair," Jim countered. "That's her

way. We should put it to the Council that they can't put a dump on her doorstep."

The meeting agreed to send a delegation to the County Council, with Jim Daly at its head, to plead Lissy's case. A "Portabeg Dumpwatch" was organised to monitor the Council's attempts to begin work. Mary Roarty – the red-faced woman – was appointed Chairperson of Dumpwatch.

Rossa stood with his cousins at their father's car.

"That was hectic stuff," Majella said.

"Sure was," Rossa agreed. "Your dad was great to bring up Lissy's case."

"It was you that started that," Majella reminded him.

"Yeh. Big hero! Big deal!" Paula said drily as she peered at the departing crowd through the gloom. "I didn't see JJ here, did you?" she asked.

"No," Majella replied. "Oh good, here's Dad. I'm freezing!" She winked at Rossa before adding, "Didn't see Bridie Doyle here either!"

Chapter Twelve

James took slow and very measured steps along the bog road. He stared downward all the time as if he were walking on a tightrope. Rossa's frustration was growing by the minute.

"Come on, James. We'll never get to see Lissy at this rate!" He turned to Margie. "Sorry about this. He's in one of his moods."

"It's OK."

"It would be OK if we had a week to make the journey. Come ON, James! *Chore! Chore! Chore!*"

The words seemed to wake James from his reverie and he quickened his step.

"Good lad, James!" Rossa rolled his eyes to heaven with relief.

"Inspiration!" Margie suggested.

"Some would call it genius!" Rossa said, with a wiggle of his head.

"Some would call what you did to JJ's bike genius – and probably foolish as well."

"Oh, you heard – "

"It was the main topic of conversation on the school bus. Have you seen JJ since?"

"No. I've been keeping out of his way."

"Bridie Doyle says he's gunning for you."

"She's the new girlfriend. Paula's gunning for me too."

"She's better off without him."

"Try telling that to her!"

Less than twenty-four hours after the protest meeting, warning signs crudely painted in red had appeared along the bog road.

LEAVE OUR BOG ALONE

DUMP OFF!

There was one official sign which had obviously been "borrowed" from elsewhere.

NO DUMPING

BY ORDER

CLARE CO COUNCIL

"Clever!" Rossa remarked.

"Well now, is that the way of it?" was Lissy's response to the news that the dump was going ahead. "Laoise, the holy woman, will have something to say about that. She'll put a curse on them."

"Uncle Jim is going to see the Council about you," Rossa reassured her.

"Well now, that's good news. I thought no one bothered about poor old Lissy."

"It was Rossa's idea," Margie said.

"Was it indeed? Well he's the *buachaill cneasta*." Lissy peered out through the broken window.

"Are you expecting someone?" Rossa asked, glad to change the subject.

"I'm watching out for Travelling Tom. I hope he hasn't forgotten me."

"Who's Travelling Tom?"

"He's the man with the travelling shop. I'd be lost without him. Well, talk of the devil, here he is at last!"

A battered blue van reversed slowly up the pathway to Lissy's house. By the time its driver had emerged from the cab, Lissy was already waiting at the rear door with a cardboard box.

"Good day to you, Lissy! You have plenty of company today!" The man removed a peaked cap to wipe his brow.

"Buon giorno, Tom. I miei cari amici."

"I never know what that stuff means, but it sure sounds musical," Tom replied as he opened the doors.

Inside the van was packed with groceries and household goods of various kinds. Tom carefully took individually wrapped eggs from Lissy's box and packed them into his own box, while Lissy chose her groceries – bread, tea, sugar, butter.

"I want something nice for my visitors," Lissy said as she fished out chocolate biscuits and a bottle of orange squash.

Travelling Tom reached further into the van and pulled out a box.

"This is what the kids are mad for."

"What are they, *in ainm Dé?*"

"Crisps. Potato crisps."

"Well they're the quare potatoes, to be sure," Lissy said, poking the packet in puzzlement. "You'd better give me half a dozen packets."

Tom took a biro from behind his ear and did a quick computation in a dog-eared notebook.

"Four pounds ten, less a pound for the eggs. We'll call it three pounds!"

"Grazie! Grazie!" Lissy said as she searched in her purse for three pound notes.

"Right so. I'll be off," Tom said as he climbed into the cab. "Are they going to put a dump beside you?" he called out.

"Not if we can help it," Rossa replied.

"That's the spirit. Though if they did, they might improve the road. This ould track has me springs ruined! See you next week, Lissy." The van wobbled its way slowly down the track.

"Arrivederci!" Lissy called out. She looked around at the blue sky that enveloped the bog. *"Che bella giornata!* I think we'll have a picnic. It's such a beautiful day!"

"Where is James?" Margie asked suddenly.

"Christ, don't tell me he's lost again," Rossa sighed.

Lissy raised a finger and beckoned them to follow her into the house. James was crouched beside a box that lay on the hearth, petting the lamb that nestled within.

"How's he doing?" Rossa asked with relief. "I had forgotten about him."

"He's coming along," Lissy said. "I thought he was gone one night last week. I sat up all night with him in my lap and he came around." She took a bottle from the dresser and gave it to James.

"Chore! Chore! Chore!" James said as he nuzzled the teat into the lamb's mouth.

Lissy, Rossa and Margie sat in the sunshine along a broken wall in the paddock. Pinkerton and Butterfly crouched on all fours in the grass, ready to pounce on any crumbs that fell to the ground.

"Well, isn't this grand?" Lissy sighed. "'Tis a long time since I had such lovely company."

Pinkerton and Butterfly, gradually emboldened, crept closer in their search for scraps. Margie suddenly jumped off the wall and raced into the house. She emerged moments later to explain.

"We forgot about poor old Siegfried. I saved him a chocolate biscuit!"

"Is James all right?" Rossa asked.

"He's *'choring'* away with the *uainín*."

Figaro was now purring in Lissy's lap. For a while nobody spoke as all three enjoyed the occasion while watching the antics of the animals. Then, unexpectedly, Lissy broke into song.

"Johnny, lovely Johnny, do you mind the day
You came to my window
To lead me away.
You said you would marry me,
Above all female kind.
Oh Johnny, lovely Johnny,
What has altered your mind?"

She paused, looked away across the bog and repeated the last two lines.

Rossa and Margie exchanged glances.

"Was there a lovely Johnny?" Rossa asked tentatively.

"Indeed there was. Indeed there was." Lissy kept her gaze fixed on the bog. "A long time ago," she added.

"What happened to him?" Margie asked.

"'Twas a long time ago. Up in Galway. I met him at a fair. He wasn't Johnny, but Andy. A fine big decent man. And kindly. Kindly, kindly." She seemed to slip into a dream-like state.

"What happened him?" Margie whispered, afraid to intrude on Lissy's reverie.

"What happened but his parents packed him off to America! They didn't want him having any truck with a gypsy woman, as they called me. He said he would come back for me one day but – I never saw him again. *Che sfortuna! Scuit!*" She swept Figaro from her lap and stood up. "I'll leave ye now. Tosca has to be milked!"

Rossa and Margie nodded to each other.

"It's time for us to be off too," Rossa said. "Thanks for the picnic!"

"Ye're welcome! I liked them crisps. I must get a packet from Travelling Tom every week. Don't forget the *uainín!*"

They parted James from the sick lamb with great difficulty. Rossa half dragged him along the track. As the trio made their way across the bog, Lissy's voice rang out in the evening air.

"Un bel di vedremo,
levarsi un fil di fumo
Sull' estremo confin del mare
E poi la nave appare . . ."

"All right, you crowd of heathens. Gather round. Fr O'Mahony will be along shortly to excommunicate the lot of you for betraying our native culture! Before that happens, we'll pick two teams, play a game of soccer and enjoy ourselves. We'll all die happy then!"

Gerry Brennan stood, hand on hips, a lean figure in a navy tracksuit amid a group of about twenty youths, clad in an assortment of jerseys, togs and tracksuits. Gerry Brennan was a physical education teacher in Limerick and a native of Liscrone. The youths gathered in a field on Gerry's father's farm.

Some soccer pitch, Rossa thought, as he surveyed a gently sloping cow-pasture which was dotted with tufts of rough grass and cowpats. He warmed to Gerry Brennan, who had an easy way with him and a sense of humour. He was also an obvious Liverpool fan.

Two teams were selected, eleven on one side and ten on the other. Rossa, on the eleven-man team, opted to play in goal.

"Right, Mr Clemence. Take the goal at the bottom of the field." He tweaked Rossa's nose. "Don't look so glum. You have The Kop behind you!"

Rossa could only laugh as he viewed the wall of brambles behind the goal. The goalposts consisted of two stakes driven into the ground.

"The crossbars haven't arrived yet. Delayed in the post!" Gerry explained. "Now, one side is a man short, so I'll give them a hand – or even a foot."

"Ah, that's not fair!" came the chorus from the eleven-man team.

"I am also the referee and I have a whistle to prove it," Gerry replied. "Any more objections? Now line up and let's get started – "

"You won't need to play with us, Mr Brennan," a red-haired boy called out. "Here comes someone else!"

All eyes turned to the figure clambering over the gate.

Rossa's heart sank. He recognised all too well the shambling gait of the burly figure that approached the group. It was JJ.

"Good God!" Gerry exclaimed. "It's Cookie Monster!"

There were giggles all around but Rossa wasn't laughing.

"Any chance of a game?" JJ asked.

"You must be joking, JJ," Gerry Brennan replied. "We're trying to start a youths' team, not a – "

"Yeh. Under-18?" the gruff voice interrupted.

"Yes, but – "

"Well I'm seventeen!"

"Stone or years? What's your mother feeding you?" asked an incredulous Gerry.

"Ah, let him play," the red-haired boy pleaded. "You were going to play with us until he came along!"

Gerry looked over the burly frame that stood before him.

"Well – all right. We'll make you a stopper. But go easy. Some of these guys are half your size! Now, could we get this game going, because unfortunately the floodlights haven't arrived either."

Rossa trooped resignedly towards his goal.

"Hey Foxie!" The voice froze him to the damp grass. "I hope you have all your spark plugs working, 'cos I'm coming to get you!"

The game got under way. It lacked any pattern, due to the players' unfamiliarity with each other – and in some cases with the rules of the game – and also to the rough terrain on which they played.

Gerry Brennan praised and censured players in turn. He was constantly cajoling and advising the boys while trying to referee the game as well.

"Good ball, Murray!"

"Spread out, lads. This isn't the cattlemart."

"Ah you can't tackle like that, you octopus!"

Rossa made some good saves, one in particular, a one-handed parry at full stretch.

"Good man, Rossa! Watch out, Ray Clemence!" Gerry shouted.

Despite his efforts, two shots beat him – one a penalty, the other a poked effort from a crowded goal mouth. What annoyed Rossa was that both goals originated from long punts by JJ. Finesse was, not surprisingly, lacking in JJ's game. Each time he got the ball, he drove it as hard as he could towards the opposing goal, despite Gerry's pleas to try passing it now and again. Rossa's team managed only one goal, thanks mainly to JJ's clumsiness and the fear of the forwards that opposed him.

When play did remain in the opposite half for a few minutes, Rossa reflected on his position. How often had he fantasised the scene.

BOY-WONDER KEEPER FOR CUP FINAL.

YOUNGEST EVER TO PLAY AT WEMBLEY.

A bizarre twist of fate has ruled out Liverpool's first, second and third-choice goalkeepers for Saturday's Cup Final against Chelsea. Manager Bill Shankly has had no option but to call up fifteen-year-old youth team keeper, Rossa Fox . . .

"Watch it, Rossa!" Gerry Brennan's call alerted him just in time. He caught the high lob cleanly and punted it upfield.

"The boy-wonder proved just that," Kenneth Wolstenholme reported on television. *"A string of miracle saves like this one – point blank – and this one – palmed onto the bar – and finally that extraordinary last minute penalty save which broke Chelsea's hearts. So it's a very*

proud fifteen-year-old Rossa Fox who skips up those famous Wembley steps to receive his cup-winner's medal – "

A shrill blast on Gerry Brennan's whistle announced half-time and brought Rossa back to reality. Reality. He smiled. Reality was a sloping damp cow-pasture in County Clare, full of thistles and grass tufts and cowpats, where there wasn't even a crossbar to palm that wonder-save onto . . .

Gerry Brennan gave a brief talk to the assembled players and they lined up for the second half. Rossa became suspicious when he saw JJ having a private word with Gerry. His fears were realised when JJ lined up for the kick-off. He had switched to centre-forward!

In the very first attack, JJ charged in heavily on Rossa, who fell back winded on the goal-line. JJ leered at him.

"I'm coming to get you, Foxie!"

Gerry Brennan whistled furiously.

"Cut that out, JJ! If you do that again, you're off!"

Fortunately for Rossa, his team maintained a sustained attack on the opposition's goal, giving him a chance to recover and frustrating JJ who bellowed at his colleagues to pass the ball to him.

Finally the ball broke upfield. It was chipped on ahead of the forward line and bobbed awkwardly towards the goal. Rossa's heart pounded. He had to go for it, but behind the ball he could see JJ, head down, charging bull-like towards the goal. It was fifty-fifty. Rossa knew if he waited on his line, the danger would be greater. JJ would simply flatten him. He dashed forward, grabbed the ball and skipped away in a sharp right turn.

JJ lunged forward, right leg outstretched. His tackle just missed Rossa, but his momentum brought him skidding through a cowpat. His foot slammed into the goalpost, upending him and causing him to cartwheel spectacularly onwards into the bramble-covered ditch.

"Jesus!" he howled. "I'm dead! I'm dead!"

"You're OK, JJ," a broadly grinning Gerry replied. "But that hedge is surely finished!"

"Me leg! Me leg! It's broken!" JJ cried.

"Come on! Give me your hand," Gerry called.

He hauled JJ out with some difficulty. JJ was in genuine pain and hobbled around until Gerry Brennan removed his boot.

"Ow! It's broken, I tell you!"

"Your big toe doesn't look too healthy," Gerry announced. "I'll bring you to Doctor Bannon. That's it, lads!" he called back to the bemused players. "Match abandoned due to unforeseen circumstances. See you next Saturday."

He looped JJ's arm around his shoulder and assisted the stumbling figure to his car. JJ turned to scowl at Rossa, his face a mass of briar scrapes. He shook his fist threateningly at the goalkeeper, who stood unmoved, still clasping the greasy football.

The boy wonder turned and held his FA Cupwinner's medal aloft to deafening roars from his delirious fans.

Chapter Thirteen

JJ's football career was temporarily suspended, much to Rossa's relief. Gerry Brennan was relieved too.

"He's more trouble than he's worth. The original bull in a china shop!"

JJ had in fact broken his big toe and spent a week hobbling around on a crutch, showing off his plastered foot and telling all who would listen how he had been the victim of a vicious tackle by "that little Belfast Provo." He won little sympathy, however, as the true story had already circulated around Liscrone. JJ was constantly teased in Lovely's Bar.

"It definitely should have been a penalty, JJ."

"Dead right, it should."

"I mean – the keeper comes out, makes no attempt to play the ball, instead he blasts your big toe with an Armalite. Definite penalty!"

Despite his handicap, JJ was back on his motorbike a week after his accident.

"You're the talk of the school bus," Margie told Rossa when they met at the old school. "They'll all be out to see you next time you're playing."

"I hope JJ doesn't turn up!"

"Don't mind him. Everybody's having a good laugh at him. He never played football before last Saturday. You should see the state of him – his foot in plaster and his face all scratched."

"Paula says that Bridie Doyle is welcome to him. She's in a terrible sulk these days, fighting with everyone." Margie was looking suspiciously around the building.

"What's up?" Rossa asked.

"Someone else has been in here," she replied.

"Well of course. Probably the farmer who stores the hay here."

"I don't think any hay has been moved." She was on her knees probing through the loose hay on the floor. "I just get a funny feeling. Look!" She pointed to a number of cigarette butts stubbed out on the stone floor.

"So? We're not the only ones who meet here!" Rossa was genuinely puzzled at her suspicions. "Someone sheltering from the rain. A courting couple. Who knows – "

"I just get a feeling. I don't know. I'm sorry. My dad says – " She stopped abruptly.

"Says what?"

"Nothing. Forget it."

"Says you should be a private investigator?" Rossa joked.

"I said forget it!"

"OK! OK!"

There was an awkward silence as they both strolled aimlessly about the building. Rossa paused to pick some of the flaking plaster from the wall.

"Do you want to hear how Uncle Jim got on with the County Council – about Lissy?"

"Of course I do." There was an acid tone to her voice, which made Rossa uneasy.

"It's not great news. They looked up the records. It seems she has no real hold on the place. She just sort of moved in there years ago. She has no whatyoumaycallit – "

"Title?"

"Yeh. No title. And as well, the dump won't actually be on her land. It will be up beyond her."

"It will still be at her back door."

"I know. But the Council say it's not their problem. It's not their fault if she moved in where she shouldn't have – "

"It's their fault to be opening a dump next door to her!"

"I know that! Look – I'm just telling you what they said. I didn't say it." He jabbed his thumbnail at the crumbling plaster. "What's got into you today? You're very touchy about everything."

"That's your opinion."

"Well you are. You're suspicious of everything – probably of me as well."

"That's not true!"

"Well, what's wrong then? Has your father been going on about me again? Maybe I should call up and show him I haven't got two heads – "

"I'm going home." Margie's voice began to tremble.

"You might as well. Everything I say seems to annoy you. And here, you might as well bring this!" He reached into his hip pocket for a folded sheet of paper and handed it to her.

Margie opened out the page and stared at it in disbelief. It was her "I am a good girl" exercise.

"Where did you get this?"

"You dropped it the day – when your schoolbag fell – the day we met."

"And you kept it all this time?"

"I didn't get a chance – I thought it might embarrass you."

"Well you should have given it back straight away. It's got nothing to do with you."

Rossa dug his hands deep into his pockets and shrugged his shoulders.

"Sorry. I didn't mean – "

"It was just a – a school thing."

She hurried out to the road without taking a precautionary look.

Rossa trudged disconsolately across the fields. He took a savage delight in beheading newly-sprouted dandelions with a swipe of his boot. First JJ. Swish. Then Paula. Swish. Then Mr Nelson. Swish. Then Margie. Sw – He paused and stepped over the dandelion. What was it with her, anyway? Something was bugging her. Maybe his cousins were right. Moody Marge. Or was it his own fault? He certainly didn't help matters by producing the "I am a good girl" page. Wrong. Wrong. Why didn't you destroy it, say nothing about it? But there was a look of horror on her face when she saw it. Not embarrassment. Horror. And it wasn't "just a school thing" like she said. You didn't get lines like that in secondary school. Still, it was stupid of him to confront her with it. Rossa. Swish.

"I've got a nice surprise for you," his mother announced over tea. "Rosaleen's taking us all to Limerick for a day's shopping."

Rossa bit into a sausage.

116

"On Saturday. She's even going to treat us to lunch. Isn't that – "

"Saturday? But I have soccer on Saturday!"

"Well you can skip it for one day."

"I can't. It's important – "

"It's important for you to get some new clothes and stuff. Look at the cut of those runners, for example."

Rossa looked at his runners. The toe-cap of one had come apart from the sole. The yellow head of a dandelion was wedged in the toe-cap.

"But Mr Brennan – "

"No more buts, Rossa. It's decided and that's that!"

There was no point in arguing. This was not going to be his day. Boy-wonder keeper. Swish.

He actually enjoyed the morning's shopping in Limerick. It was good to be back in a city again, particularly one free of soldiers and roadblocks. If only he didn't have to miss soccer practice. And if only he didn't have to wear that hideous purple and green jumper . . . At least the new runners were OK.

Lunch in a restaurant. When did he last have lunch in a restaurant? He remembered being brought by Wesley Smyth's parents to celebrate Wesley's tenth birthday. When was that? Six years ago? Six hundred years ago?

Ten past one. He would never make soccer practice now.

"Come on, James! You like sausages and beans," his mother coaxed.

James hid his face in his hands and resolutely refused to touch his food.

"Auntie Rosaleen will be very upset – "

James shook his head and began to emit strange high-pitched sounds.

"James! Stop that at once!" His mother's tone changed from cajoling to annoyance.

James replied with a full-throated scream and swept the plate of sausages and beans onto the floor. A shocked silence fell on the restaurant before Maureen Fox knelt down to clear up the mess.

"I'm sorry about this," she said to the waitress. "We're leaving now."

They wandered along the street, Maureen and her sister pausing occasionally to gaze into fashion boutique windows. Boring, Rossa thought. Further up the street he noticed a man unlocking his car. It was Michael Nelson. Without thinking Rossa ran towards him.

"Mr Nelson?"

"Yes?"

"My name is Rossa Fox."

"I know that."

"Would you be going home to Portabeg now?"

"I might be."

"Would you – could I have a lift?"

Michael Nelson was clearly taken aback at this request.

"Well, I suppose – "

"Thanks. I'll be back in a second!"

He sprinted back to his mother.

"Mum, can I go home now with Mr Nelson?"

"Indeed you cannot – "

"Please, Mum, you've got all my stuff – "

"Let him go, Maureen," his aunt intervened. "I won't be offended!"

"Well – "

"Thanks, Mum. I'll see you later. Thanks, Aunt Rosaleen." He tore back up the street where Michael Nelson sat impatiently drumming his fingertips on the steering-wheel of his car.

It was only when he sat into the car that Rossa realised how reckless he had been. He had acted totally on impulse. He would surely have to endure either a frosty silence or a forty-minute lecture now. Rossa did his best to break the ice.

"We were shopping all morning."

"I see."

"It's a fine city, Limerick."

"It is that."

"I have soccer practice this afternoon and Mammy wasn't finished shopping, so that's why I asked for a lift."

"I see."

"Do you know Mr Brennan, the soccer coach?"

"I think I know the family."

Michael Nelson switched on the car radio. Rossa remained silent for a while, and then tried a change of subject.

"Did Uncle Jim tell you about seeing the Council – about the dump – and Lissy?"

"I heard he didn't have much luck."

"They can't build a dump at Lissy's back door." He remembered that that was how Margie had described it.

"Would she notice the difference?"

"That's not a nice thing to say, Mr Nelson. We were up there and – "

"We?" The question was like a rifle shot.

Rossa retrieved the situation just in time.

"M-me and James – my wee brother. She's a real nice lady when you get to know her."

"Indeed."

Rossa found his confidence rising.

"You don't like me, do you, Mr Nelson?"

"I hardly know you."

"Yeh, but you don't like me. You don't like me being with Margie – "

"Look! All I know is that you came from doubtful circumstances in Belfast. I don't want Margie getting into trouble. Margie's a good girl and I want her to stay a good girl. Is that clear?"

The phrase stunned Rossa. A good girl. I am a good girl. Now he knew . . .

"I said, 'Is that clear?'"

"Yeah, that's clear."

There was silence for the rest of the journey.

Brennan's Field showed a number of improvements on Rossa's second visit. The wooden stakes had been replaced by metal goal-frames, most of the grass tufts had been cut and the playing-area had been crudely lined with limestone.

"The floodlights are still delayed, lads," Gerry Brennan announced, "and there's no sign of the showers either. We'll start off with some dribbling and passing practice."

Eventually the group was again divided into two teams and once again Rossa played in goal.

Whenever play drifted upfield, Rossa reflected on his drive home from Limerick with Michael Nelson. He shuddered at the thought of his own bravado. It was almost as if he were looking into the car at another person. Was that really him saying, "You don't like me, do you, Mr Nelson?" And then, "Margie's a good girl . . ."

Something whistled past his left ear.

"Dreaming, Rossa, Beddy-byes! You should have come out for that one," Gerry shouted. Rossa turned shamefacedly to retrieve the ball from the hedge.

"You let in three goals?" his mother said. "I told you you should have stayed in Limerick! Now would you put an egg on to boil for your brother there." She turned to the bin in the corner.

"Naughty brother that disgraced us all in Limerick!"

"Mind you don't drop that egg, Rossa, with the kind of form you're in today," she called.

The day out certainly suited you, Rossa thought.

The door burst open and Rosaleen rushed in. "The television!" she called out. "Put on the television!"

Rossa pressed the button.

"God, Rosaleen. You put the heart crossways in me!" Maureen cried. "What in God's name – ?"

"Shush!"

The newsreader's voice broke through.

"– a major breakout from Long Kesh prison. Initial reports suggest that at least six men had escaped. Authorities have yet to confirm that the group includes Provisional IRA bomber Patrick Fox, who was recently sentenced to twenty years' imprisonment."

"Jesus, Mary and Joseph," Maureen Fox whispered.

The egg slipped through Rossa's fingers and burst into a mess on the floor.

Chapter Fourteen

Subsequent bulletins confirmed Maureen Fox's fears.

"He'll not come near us. He doesn't know where we are. He wouldn't dare, even if he did know." She addressed the words to Rossa but he knew she was trying to reassure herself more than him. She bought three Sunday newspapers and read the accounts of the escape closely.

"Thank God there's no mention of us. I hope it stays that way. We'll just have to be on our guard."

When a knock came to the door of the mobile home that evening, Maureen Fox and her elder son froze and exchanged anxious looks. It was Sergeant Fogarty.

"You know why I'm here, Mrs Fox. We're just making routine enquiries. Have you – ?"

"No, we've seen or heard nothing, only what's on the television or in the papers. I don't want any truck with him. I'm just trying to get on with my life down here."

"Well, if you notice anything or if you're worried, get in touch with us. That applies to this young man too," he added, turning towards Rossa.

That night Rossa took down the biscuit-tin from the top of the wardrobe and searched again for his First Communion photograph. He studied it for a long time. The father he knew then. Would he know him now, if he showed up? If he did show up, what would he himself do? Would he "get in touch", as Sergeant Fogarty had suggested?

The mother who looked not much older than Paula. Smiling. Happy. And the shy little blond girl by her side . . . Please don't let this start the nightmare again. As he replaced the photograph, he noticed Margie's letter on top of the pile. What would she think? Her father would probably lock her up altogether now, just to ensure she remained "a good girl".

"Crips! Crips! Crips!" James chanted.

"I haven't got any crisps, so don't be annoying me!" Rossa shouted at his brother. "You've been going on all morning – "

"Lovely! Lovely! Lovely!" James screamed.

"I haven't got any money, so there's no point going on about that either!"

He knew his words would have little effect. As the argument continued, James grew increasingly boisterous and began up-ending chairs on the kitchen floor.

"Jesus, James! Sometimes I'd love to put you in that bin and just sit on the lid until you – until you shut up!"

Rossa began a furious search among jars and jugs on the top shelf of the kitchen dresser. His mother had a habit of putting loose change there to help pay the milkman's bill each week.

"Crips! Crips! Crips!" The chant became more grating on Rossa's ears.

"I'm looking! I'm looking!" His search turned up a mere eighteen pence.

"Come on!" he barked at James. "We're going for your blasted 'crips'."

"Lovely! Lovely! Lovely!" James replied.

The Battery Lynch sat on a high stool at the grocery counter in Lovely's. He was munching a bag of crisps and took a long drink from a pint glass of lemonade. He raised the glass in salute to Rossa and James.

"Good men! Hurl them, Portabeg!"

Rossa smiled nervously in return. To his astonishment, Margie emerged from the gloom of the bar beyond. They each half-turned away in embarrassment but both knew there was no escape.

"Hi!" Rossa blurted. "I – just came in for crips – sorry, crisps – for this fellow. He has me pestered all morning. Are you not at school?"

Brilliant question. Brilliantly stupid.

"No. I had to get a message for Daddy."

"Is he – ?"

"H-he works at home sometimes. I have to help him."

"Beats school any day!" Rossa joked.

There was no reply.

"Did he tell you – he met me?"

"Yeh. Said he gave you a lift. He said you were a cheeky youngster."

Rossa blushed. He noticed a faint smile on Margie's face. The ice was breaking.

"I suppose he was right. I was in a rush home for soccer practice – "

"How did you get on?"

"Let in three goals. Should have stayed in Limerick!"

Lovely emerged from the bar area, wrapping something in newspaper.

"Lovely! Lovely! Lovely!" he muttered.

"Crips! Crips! Crips!" James sang.

"Come on the beggars!" The Battery added with a nod of his head.

Rossa rolled his eyes upwards.

"The three of them should be in a band together," he whispered.

"Now, Miss." Lovely handed the parcel to Margie who proffered a five-pound note in return.

"Lovely! Lovely! Lovely!" he said as he foraged in the tray for change.

"Crips! Crips! – "

"Oh all right, James! Would you like a bag of crisps?" Rossa asked Margie.

"OK." She accepted the change from Lovely.

"Two bags of crisps, please – " As he said the words, Rossa realised with horror that he wouldn't have enough money. He began a frantic search of his pockets.

"I have money if you're – "

"No. I have, I mean I thought – "

Liar. Liar. He began to count the money, knowing well what the total would be.

"Twenty pence. Lovely! Lovely! Lovely!"

"I'm afraid I can only find eighteen – "

Margie dropped twopence into his cupped palm. Twit! Absolute twit!

"Thanks! Don't know what happened – "

Do know. Liar.

"Hurl them, Portabeg!" The Battery shouted.

James tucked into his crisps as they retreated to the window.

"I heard about your father," Margie whispered.

Rossa shrugged his shoulders. "Hope he doesn't come this way."

"I'm – sorry about the last time," Margie said. "I – wasn't feeling well."

"It's OK. I wasn't much help myself."

"Cheeky!"

"Yeh!"

Boy-wonder keeper flings his body to the left and makes an unbelievable save . . .

"We're playing our first match on Saturday. Against Ard-na-gur – "

She giggled at his mispronunciation.

"Ard na GUN!" she corrected him.

"It's only a friendly. Mr Brennan wants to see how good – or bad – Portabeg are – "

"Hurl them, Portabeg!" The Battery interjected.

"Will you be – can you come?"

"Don't know. I'll see. I have to go now. Good luck on Saturday. See you, James!"

James was busily poking the last crisp crumbs out of the corner of the bag.

"More crips! More crips! More – "

"You must be joking, James. That's your lot!" Rossa warned his brother.

"Here!" Margie pressed a tenpenny piece into Rossa's hand. "He can have a bag on me." She had left the shop before he could react.

When he turned the corner from Lowney's, Rossa

found the road almost totally blocked by a huge low-loader. He was so intrigued by it that he almost stumbled into a dark-blue car that was parked in the shadow of Lowney's gable end. Two men sitting in the front eyed him, unsmiling and silent. They were strangers to Rossa, but their gaze unsettled him.

"Come on, James!"

"Tractor! Tractor!" James stood transfixed by the activity that unfurled before them. A large earth-moving machine was slowly manoeuvred from the low-loader and was then used to off-load a timber-framed workmen's hut. The hut was then positioned at the end of the grassy track that led to Portabeg Wood and the bog beyond. The earth-mover occupied the full width of the track as it began to scrape the grassy surface away and tear out the hedges on either side. Work was starting on the dump.

"Come on, James!" Rossa tugged at his brother's arm. "We have to tell people."

He glanced back at the car. The two men were still watching.

People in Portabeg did not need to be told what was happening. The arrival of the low-loader triggered instant reaction among the local community. Mary Roarty's Dumpwatch Committee met at lunchtime and by early afternoon a sit-down was organised on the track where the earth-mover had begun working. Michael Nelson was seen having words with the driver of the earth-mover. He shrugged his shoulders, turned off the engine, got into his car and drove off to loud cheers from the protesters.

"Round One to us!" Mary Roarty shouted to renewed cheers from her colleagues. As Rossa joined in the cheering, he noticed the dark-blue car, still occupied, at Lowney's gable end.

A hastily convened meeting in Liscrone National School that evening arranged a rota of volunteers for the sit-down protest. Placards were distributed and Michael Nelson and Jim Daly were deputed to see the County Council's officials again.

Overnight, Lissy became the focus of the protest. Placards proclaimed warnings:

LEAVE LISSY ALONE

PORTABEG SUPPORTS LISSY

Rossa gave a wry smile. A month ago there hadn't been much support for her. Now everybody loved her.

The protest grew in intensity. Numbers on the sit-in increased as the community's confidence grew. Graffiti appeared on the workmen's hut.

NO PLANNING PERMISSION FOR THIS.

DUMP IT!

For two days the earth-mover driver turned up, sat in his cab, read the newspaper, drank tea from a flask and then left to applause and raucous cheering from the protesters.

On the third day, the County Council decided to take on the protesters. Sergeant Fogarty arrived, followed by a squad car from which three gardaí emerged. The sergeant read an official notice about "unlawful assembly and obstruction" and asked the protesters to move. He was greeted with a stony silence.

"I'm sorry, folks, but I have my duty to do." He nodded to the three gardaí and together they began to remove the protesters forcibly. There were howls of pain and complaint as the protesters locked arms together in an effort to hold their position.

"Ow!"

"Bully boys!"

"Nazis!"

"Traitors! Whose side are you on?"

Slowly, the gardaí cleared a path through the protesters and dragged them around behind the earth-mover. The driver switched on the engine. The huge machine shuddered and began to inch forward at first and then, as the path was cleared, its great caterpillar wheels picked up speed. The protesters watched in anguish, held back by the gardaí.

Mary Roarty could not contain her anger. She suddenly wrenched herself free from the garda's grip and gave a loud shriek as she chased after the earth-mover and attempted to clamber towards the driver's cab.

The driver, intent on proceeding now that he had got started, was oblivious to her efforts. Her voice was drowned by the noise of the machine. Just as she seemed to have reached the cab, the machine lurched violently to one side and Mary Roarty tumbled down onto the caterpillar track. Her body was juggled along the track. A chorus of shrieks broke out from the horrified watching group.

Sergeant Fogarty reacted more quickly than anyone else. He sprinted after the machine, somehow forced his way alongside through the churned-up earth and, at the last minute, grabbed Mary's arm and yanked her clear of the grinding wheel. The driver looked aghast at the two bodies that were tossed into the ditch and instantly switched off the machine.

For a moment an eerie silence fell on the group and then panic erupted. People rushed forward to Mary's aid, while one garda raced back to the squad car to summon an ambulance. Sergeant Fogarty struggled to his feet, shaken but unhurt. Mary Roarty lay unconscious in the ditch, her clothes in tatters, her arms and legs a mass of lacerations. There were loud cries of anguish as her fellow-protesters tried to make her comfortable with coats and blankets. It seemed to take an age for the ambulance to arrive but, when it did and Mary was carefully eased onto a stretcher and then into the ambulance, a weird and unnatural silence fell on Portabeg. Rossa, who only arrived for the latter part of the drama, stood with James and watched as the participants melted away in a stunned silence. The only people who did not seem affected by the morning's events were the two men sitting in the dark-blue car at Lowney's gable.

Chapter Fifteen

The injuries to Mary Roarty cast an initial gloom over Portabeg but that gloom gave way to anger and an even firmer resolve, especially when Mary was well enough to issue instructions from her hospital bed. Once she had regained consciousness, her diagnosis was not as bad as it had first seemed. A broken collar-bone, some severe bruising and a lot of abrasions were not enough to quell Mary's fire.

"Round Two to us!" was her first message to the Dumpwatch Committee.

She was correct. The County Council agreed to halt the clearance work until tempers abated. The sit-downs were suspended, but the truce was uneasy. One morning, the residents on their way to work and school discovered that a half-mile of road had been crudely daubed in white paint with NO DUMP HERE slogans. The County Council eventually called for a meeting with representatives of the Portabeg community, having earlier heard Jim Daly and Michael Nelson plead Lissy's case. Meanwhile, the earth-mover stood where it had stopped the day Mary Roarty won Round Two of the Dump War.

About fifty people turned up to watch Portabeg United's first match against Ardnagun. They were mostly parents and families of the players, with a few curious onlookers who came to witness the "foreign game" that Fr O'Mahony had grudgingly announced from the altar.

Rossa was selected to play in goal. The team wore a motley collection of jerseys in contrast to Ardnagun, who were neatly kitted out in a green and white strip.

Gerry Brennan noticed his team's envious looks at the opposition.

"Don't mind the fancy gear, lads. It's what you do with the ball that matters." He gave the team a last-minute pep talk. Rossa scanned the straggle of spectators. He was pleased to see his mother among them, firmly holding James's hand. He was even more pleased to observe the slight figure of Margie entering the field.

"Dreaming again, Rossa!" Gerry Brennan's sharp voice broke in on his reverie. "Dreaming time is over. Go out there and do your best. And remember – play with your heads, as well as your feet – and I'm not talking about heading the ball!"

As Rossa made his way to the goal at the bottom of the slope, he was disquieted to see the hunched figure of JJ, together with Bridie Doyle, taking up a position near the goal. As soon as the match started, JJ began his invective.

"Watch it, Foxie, the SAS are coming!"

"You're going to get knee-capped – first ball that comes in . . ."

Ardnagun started like a whirlwind. Using both the wind and the slope, together with their obvious experience, they cut through the Portabeg defence. Rossa was kept busy and within five minutes he was retrieving the ball from the hedge. One-nil to Ardnagun.

"Come on, Foxie! Me granny would have stopped that one!" JJ teased.

"Settle down, lads! Settle down!" Gerry Brennan called from the touch-line.

As Portabeg prepared to kick off again, Rossa heard angry exchanges to his right. His mother was upbraiding JJ.

"Whose side are you on anyway?" The Belfast accent echoed across the field, initially embarrassing Rossa. "Leave him alone! He's doing his best. Be off with you now!"

JJ moved sheepishly away, to the sniggers of those nearby. Rossa felt a surge of pride and shook his fist in a gesture of support.

Gradually Portabeg settled and gained in confidence. In the second half, they pressed forward relentlessly and were eventually rewarded when Georgie Doyle, Bridie's brother, drove home an equaliser, to the delight of the small group of supporters. Then five minutes from the end, disaster struck Portabeg. Ardnagun made a rare attack and when there was little evident danger, their centre-forward was brought down. Penalty.

The boy-wonder adjusted his cap as both the blinding sun and the Chelsea penalty-taker bore down on him. In the distance, a sudden glint momentarily distracted him. The sun had caught Princess Margie's tiara in the Royal Box. He took it as a signal. He would do it for her, not for the grumpy old King beside her, but for her – and Liverpool, of course. The crescendo of noise was frightening. Cheers, boos, whistles. Thump! He flung his body towards the top right-hand corner. It seemed as if the effort would tear his ribs apart but he stretched those extra inches. He would do it – for her. He felt his fingertips make contact with the stinging leather and, as he fell, he watched the gleaming ball spin upwards and over the bar.

His body hit the damp grass heavily.

"Brilliant save, Rossa!"

He could detect Gerry Brennan's voice above the din. He had done it – for Portabeg.

"One-all. A great result. Well done, lads. We're on our way!" Gerry Brennan moved excitedly among his players, congratulating them individually. "Clemence would have been proud of that one!" he whispered to Rossa.

"You were brilliant, Rossa. I'm right proud of you. Aren't we, James?" His mother gave him a big hug.

"Mum! Everyone's watching!" Rossa squirmed with embarrassment.

"You were great," Margie said.

"I was busy enough anyway!" Rossa replied, digging the toe of his boot into the soft turf.

"Daddy's going to the big hurling match in Limerick tomorrow. I could meet you at the old school, around two o'clock."

"Great!"

The boy-wonder bowed politely to the princess before going on to receive his medal from the dour-faced king. As he took the medal, he kissed it and gave an impish wink to the princess.

"Cheeky!" the King grunted.

"There's ice cream for dessert. Can you not wait?" his mother pleaded.

"I'll – have it later. I have to go now."

"Where?"

"Just out."

"Where out?"

"I won't be that long. Bye."

"Take care, Rossa. You know – "

The door slammed.

"Must be love, James," his mother sighed. James slapped his ice cream hard with a spoon.

"Come on the beggars!" he growled.

Rossa dribbled an imaginary ball along the headland. There was a pleasant heat in the day – enough to warrant shedding the purple and green jumper and hiding it in the hedge until his return. Things were looking up. He had played well and his mum was proud of him. *Body swerve – oh yes, dodged that tackle beautifully.* They were winning the Dump War, it seemed. *Look up, hit a perfect forty-yard crossfield pass. Such vision!* Margie and he were on good terms. He wished the afternoon would crawl by like the morning had done. *Take the return pass. Hit it on the volley, knee-high. Goal!*

He reached the old schoolhouse at Bawnmore. He glanced at his watch. Five to two. No sign of her. He would play a trick on her. Bury himself in the hay and surprise her. He made a run and dived into the hay.

"Jesus!" A voice shrieked from the far corner of the building.

A startled Rossa sprang backwards into a standing position as a tall, lean figure emerged from the gloom and moved menacingly towards him.

"Jesus Christ! Rossa!"

Rossa Fox found himself staring with incredulity into the bearded, gaunt face of his father.

Chapter Sixteen

"Jesus Christ, Rossa – what are you doing here?"

"I-I could ask you the same question." Rossa caught a glimpse of grey steel as his father quickly slipped something into the inside pocket of his jacket and hurriedly zipped up the fly of his trousers.

"I could have plugged you – would have, only I was having a pee," he added with a nervous laugh. "Are you on your own?" The voice became edgy again.

"Yes – no!" He glanced at his watch. Two o'clock. "There's someone else coming – a friend."

"Up! Quick!" his father snapped, motioning towards a ladder that stood vertically in the centre of the floor. "Come on!" His father jabbed him towards the ladder. On his previous visits to the school, Rossa had never noticed the loft that had been created in one half of the building, probably because the hay had been stacked tightly up to the false ceiling. As his head came above the level of the ceiling and his eyes became more accustomed to the gloom, he found himself gaping open-mouthed at what was, in essence, a secret den, the kind of private place he would love to have for himself –

"Would you move? Christ, you were always a dreamer!"

He crawled into the loft. It was spacious but confined in height, as Rossa discovered when he tried to stand up and cracked his head against a beam. His father bundled him towards the gable wall and then hastily and silently hauled up the ladder and laid it flat on the floor of the loft. His father crept on all fours towards Rossa.

"Now. Not a word. Not a whisper. Not a move until your friend has come – and gone!"

It was weird. Sitting there in the half-light, back to the gable wall, beside – almost touching – the man who was his father, hearing only their quiet breathing. As they waited, Rossa observed how well the loft had been prepared for its visitor. A sleeping-bag, blankets, primus stove, large torch, a box of food, several cans of beer, even a small stack of books.

It was strange how, when you remained perfectly still, you could hear the slightest noise – a small bird pattering across the roof, something small scurrying across the floor in the corner, a breeze rustling through the leaves of a tree outside. Rossa's heart quickened when he detected a brushing through the long grass outside. She was here! His father knew it too. He gripped Rossa's arm tightly, so tightly that the boy winced in pain and tugged away. His father relaxed the grip and glowered at Rossa, his dark features mute and menacing. Footsteps on concrete now. Stillness. Suddenly a voice calling his name in a loud whisper. The grip on his arm tightened again.

A sigh, just below him. Pacing to and fro. Silence. Movement again. Outside now. Please go, Rossa prayed. I don't want you involved. Go. To his horror, she entered the building. He could hear her sit down on the hay. Don't look up. Go, please. He was almost afraid to breathe. He could hear the ticking of his watch. If this went on, she would hear it too. At last, after what seemed an eternity, she stood up, brushed the loose hay from her clothes, gave a prolonged sigh and left.

His father waited a few minutes before speaking.

"What a place to pick as a hideaway! It's like Central Station! Anyway, what in hell's name are you doing in this part of the world?"

"You obviously know or you wouldn't be here – "

"Look, sunshine, you are positively the last person in the entire world I expected to see coming in that door today. Believe me!"

"We moved down here after – " He paused as the painful memories came back to him.

"After what?"

"After they burned us out."

"Bastards. Bloody Proddy bastards!"

"It was because of you they did it."

"Because of me? That's rich. That lot don't need an excuse. Whose side are you on, anyway?" He knelt up, crawled over to the sleeping bag and fumbled for a packet of cigarettes. He offered one to Rossa who shook his head. His father lit a cigarette and inhaled deeply. As he blew the smoke towards a gap in the slates above, he laughed quietly to himself.

"There's no doubt! Reminds me of Humphrey Bogart in that old film. Of all the bars in all the world, I had to walk into this one!" He shook his head in disbelief. "Tell us. How is herself?"

"Her name is Maureen."

"Well you've turned right cheeky!"

You're the second one to call me that, Rossa thought.

"How is Maureen, then?" his father asked with mock politeness.

"She's OK. She has a job – in a big house – five mornings a week."

"Well isn't that grand for her. And who minds the wee fella – James?" he added quickly before Rossa corrected him.

"I do!"

"Are you not at school?"

"Not yet. Mum's trying to organise it for September."

"That's hardly good enough, is it?"

Rossa pretended not to hear that remark.

Another long draw on the cigarette.

"So, how come you're down here?"

"Auntie Rosaleen lives a couple of miles away – "

"I thought she lived in Limerick."

"They moved out here. Built a new house. We're in their mobile home."

"It's a small world and no mistake," his father said. "Of all the bars . . . So. How are you?"

"I'm OK. I'm the goalkeeper in the local soccer team. We drew our first game yesterday. One-all. I saved a penalty!" he said in a sudden burst of enthusiasm.

"Did ye now? Soccer? Down here?"

"They're just starting."

"And you're courtin', I see?"

"She's just a friend."

"Come on, Rossa! You don't meet a friend in a hayshed!"

"Her father doesn't like me."

139

"Hah! History repeats itself! Your mother – Maureen's – father didn't like me either!" He reached back for a can of beer. "Want a swig?"

"No, thanks."

His father took a long drink from the can.

"You're well provided for here," Rossa observed drily.

"Oh indeed! My friends down here are looking after me all right!" He waved his arm in a sweeping gesture. "Look at this! It's nearly as good as the Kesh, for God's sake!"

There was a long silence.

"Why did you do it, Dad?" Rossa asked.

"Do what?"

"Break out."

Patrick Fox looked at his son with growing incredulity.

"You're something else, you know that? Sure why would I want to break out of the Kesh – and me a guest of Her Majesty, with all the comforts of home and privileges like family visits – only my family never bothered to visit me! Sure I must be out of my tree, out of my fu– . . . ah, give me a break, will you?"

"We could hardly visit when we didn't live up there any more."

"If you lived outside the gates of the Kesh, you still wouldn't visit me! Oh it was a real picnic, all right!"

"You were in there for a reason." Rossa found that his father's attitude was emboldening him.

"Oh, Mammy has little Rossa in her grip all right." He squashed the empty beer-can viciously. "Hasn't she? I was in there because I was doing what had to be done. There's a war going on up there, in case you didn't notice. A war that was necessary after years, hundreds of

140

years, of repression, domination and discrimination. A people can only take so much. We didn't start it but, by God, we'll finish it! We'll take the struggle to the Brits – on their own territory if necessary. We'll not leave it to the namby-pambies like you!"

Rossa felt the tears burning a furrow down his cheeks. His father tore open another can of beer. Rossa's sniffling punctuated another long silence. His father's tone suddenly mellowed.

"Look, son. Maybe I was a namby too as a young fellow. But I remember my father being beaten to a pulp by a gang of drunken Orange louts on their way back from a 'Twelfth' parade. All because he had a few drinks and shouted 'Fuck the sash me father wore!' at them. That changed me, I can tell you. Maybe someday you'll see your father in a different light – "

"I do."

"How so?"

"I see a father who used to be at home, who used to play football with me, push me on a swing – "

"Ah that's grand dreamy stuff. But you can't eat dreams. What about the father that lost his job because he was the wrong colour? Green, not orange. And because he was unemployed, he was suspected of everything. So he said, 'Frig it, if they feel like that, I'll give them something to suspect me of. Enough is enough.' Of course – I'd love to be playing football with you. Taking penalties and all. But things have to be put right first."

"With bombs?"

"If needs be, yes."

"You didn't ask about Sophie?"

"What do you mean, Sophie? She's dead, isn't she?"

"Yeh, from a bomb."

"Look, don't lay that on me! Don't think it didn't tear the heart out of me. I still have nightmares about Sophie. I was crazy about her. But she was a casualty of war. Just because some Loyalist nut couldn't prime a bomb properly. She was in the wrong place at the wrong time. Who let her up there anyway?"

Rossa could see nothing but glass exploding. Huge shards of glass, spearing towards –

"I-have-to-go," he stammered.

"How do you know I'll let you?" his father snapped. "Joke! Joke!" he added quickly. "Go if you want to – but remember you can't run away all the time."

"Neither can you!"

His father replied by taking up the ladder and lowering it silently.

"There you are. You're free to go. Freedom is a wonderful thing, Rossa. You were named after a man who valued freedom – and gave his life for it. O'Donovan Rossa."

Rossa began his descent.

"Just remember. You saw nothing, heard nothing. Did you?" The menacing tone had returned to his father's voice.

As he hauled the ladder up again, he called out, "Good luck, Rossa. I'll be moving on myself. Too hot around here. Think about what I said. And keep saving the penalties!"

Rossa slipped out furtively and hurried back across the fields to Portabeg. He welcomed the fine drizzle that cooled his burning eyes.

Of course he hadn't seen his father. Not for five years. Wouldn't recognise him, probably. He hadn't got a father, had he? You must be thinking of someone else . . .

The drizzle saturated his T-shirt. Just in time, he remembered the purple and green jumper. He retrieved it from the hedge and pulled it on over the wet T-shirt.

Chapter Seventeen

"We're watching a film on your telly. Your Mum and James are gone for a walk. Hope you don't mind!" Majella stretched herself full-length on the settee.

Mind? Of course I bloody mind. You're the last people I wanted to see.

"Where's Paula?" Rossa asked.

"In there." She nodded towards the kitchenette. "Making the coffee."

Make yourself at home, he thought. Would you like some biscuits, cream cake, chocolate gateau?

Paula entered with two mugs of coffee.

"Couldn't find any bickies. Hello!" She threw the last remark at Rossa. "Shove over, Jelly. You can't have the whole place to yourself."

"Heard you were brilliant in the match, Rossa," Majella said. "Saved a penalty and all."

Rossa shrugged his shoulders. The room was stifling him. A blaring television on one side, two boisterous cousins on the other.

"Heard Auntie Maureen was brilliant too," Majella continued. "Sent JJ packing. Bridie Doyle was furious!"

"Shush, Jelly!" Paula snapped. "The film is starting. There's Ryan O'Neal. God, he's gorgeous!"

"He'd remind you of JJ." Majella persisted with her provocation.

"Would you ever shut up, Jelly. That chapter of my life is closed," she added haughtily as she reached across to turn up the volume. In doing so, she glanced at Rossa. "What happened you? You look like you've seen a ghost!"

"Yeh," Majella agreed. "You're as white as a sheet."

"Or was it the moody one you saw?" Paula teased. "She went down the road on the bike half an hour ago, and she'd freeze hell over with a look!"

"Bitch!" Rossa spat the word at her as he left the room and slammed the door behind him.

"Oh lovely. There's Saint Rossa for you now!" Paula called after him.

He sank slowly onto James's duvet. The reality of the last hour's events was only now sinking in. His father, escaped prisoner, Provo bomber, killer, was in hiding two miles away. Killer, killer, killer. What should he do? Tell his mother? She'd go bananas. "Get in touch" with Sergeant Fogarty? Killer, killer, killer. Father, father, father. "I'll be moving on. It's too hot around here." Move on, then. Now.

A scraping sound to his right distracted him. Rocky the terrapin was attempting to scale the side of his tank. I know how you feel, Rocky, Rossa thought.

Another argument was developing in the television room. At least you can shrink back under your shell . . .

The earth-mover had now become a focal point in the Dump War. It was festooned with bunting and protest placards. Someone had positioned a huge teddy bear, dressed in the Portabeg hurling colours of red and white, in the driver's seat. Graffiti were sprayed around the driver's cab:

PORTABEG 2, COUNTY COUNCIL 0

NO SURRENDER!

MARY ROARTY RULES!

Rossa surveyed the scene with some amusement. He had strolled up to the site, ostensibly to have a look at Portabeg's latest attraction, but had timed his stroll to coincide with the arrival of the school bus. The squabble of boisterous voices, punctuated by occasional shrieks and bouts of name-calling, told him his timing was perfect. He moved back down the ploughed-up track to the road. The straggle of students, swinging schoolbags, arguing and chasing each other, passed by. No sign of Margie. He dug his hands into his pockets and turned to follow them.

"She's in Lovely's!" Majella called back to him.

"Thanks!" he shouted and tried not to seem hurried as he doubled back to the shop. Beeny Flynn was having her customary argument with Lovely, who was struggling with the bacon-slicer.

"Don't cut them rashers so thick this time. And the last lot I got were as salty as the Atlantic Ocean. I was drinking water by the gallon all week!"

"Oh lovely, lovely, lovely. As lovely a bit of bacon as you'll find. I had a bit of it for my dinner yesterday."

"That bit looks very fatty. I don't like fat. It upsets my stomach. Have you not got a leaner bit?"

"Lovely, lovely, lovely – "

Rossa was glad of the diversion and the delay. He approached nervously.

"Hi!"

"Hi." She seemed equally nervous.

"I'm sorry about yesterday," he began. "I – couldn't make it. Something came up – about my father – " He was never a convincing liar. What if she had seen him returning across the fields?

"It's OK. I guessed something had happened."

He felt the relief drain through his body.

"Did you – stay long?"

"Not really. It turned out lucky. I had only got back home when Daddy rang. His car broke down on the way to Limerick. I had to go down to Reilly's Garage with a message. He couldn't get through to them on the phone."

"Close shave."

"Yeh. He came back home, rather than go to the match. Just as well. Clare were walloped!"

Beeny was driving a hard bargain.

"You might as well throw in that end bit for luck! Sure it would be no use to anyone else – "

Margie looked anxiously at her watch.

"I'll be murdered. Daddy's waiting on cigarettes. He's at home today. No car."

"I suppose you won't get up to the old school for a while," Rossa said hopefully. Not until he "moves on" . . .

"I don't think it's a good place to meet any more."

"Oh?"

"I got a queer feeling there yesterday. And I saw bits of plaster on the floor."

"Maybe the walls are collapsing." It was a weak attempt at humour.

"No. Not that kind of plaster. Plaster of Paris. The white stuff. I think JJ could have been there."

"JJ? What would he be doing there?"

"Ask Bridie Doyle! Anyway it might be better to stay away from there – for a while."

"Yeh! Suppose you're right." He was floating above a sea of relief.

Beeny had finished her business at last. Margie got her cigarettes and rushed to the door.

"I have to run. I'll see you." The bell above the door jangled noisily. She paused. "By the way, there's a meeting about the dump on Wednesday night. Daddy thinks it could be troublesome."

"Why?"

"Don't know. 'Bye!"

"'Bye! Oh – the plaster of Paris – that was brilliant!" he called as she skipped away. She acknowledged with a wave of her hand and was gone.

Rossa stood on Lowney's doorstep and reflected on how well things had turned out. Across the road, the dark-blue car was parked outside Reilly's Garage. He could only see the driver, as the other passenger had a newspaper opened out in front of him. The driver was staring at him. Rossa felt distinctly uneasy as he turned the corner for home.

The uneasiness continued over the next couple of days. His mother noticed it.

"You're awful quiet. Is there anything wrong?"

"No. Why should there be?"

"Just asking. Are you worried about your father?"

"W-what do you mean?"

"Where he is. What's happening to him."

"Suppose so."

"He's crazy to do what he did. I just hope he's not crazy enough to come down here."

"Why – would he do that?"

"To see you. To see James. Maybe even to see me." She gave a nervous chuckle. "We're still his family, in the end of all."

"But you don't want to see him?"

"No. I can't take what he stands for. Not . . . after Sophie . . ." She lit a cigarette hurriedly.

"What would you do – if he came to see you?"

"Jesus, Rossa, don't even mention it. I'd freak out."

"But you said we're still his family – "

"In name. And look where that name has got us. That fellow taunting you at the match. The letter – "

"What letter?"

"I shouldn't have mentioned that – "

"What letter?" Rossa persisted.

"It was nothing. Just one of those cowardly anonymous ones."

"What did it say?"

"It doesn't matter, Rossa. I burned it. I don't even remember it. End of story."

Of course I remember, she thought. It's burned into my memory.

Provo-fucker.

Take your Provo son and your spastic and get to hell out of here. We don't want your kind around here. You have been warned.

She hadn't burned it, but had given it to Sergeant Fogarty. He had his suspicions but said nothing. Two weeks had elapsed. Nothing had happened.

"I had a letter of a different kind today," she said, glad to change the subject.

"Oh?"

"From Drumroe School. The principal wants to see us in two weeks' time."

"What about?"

"You know what about, Rossa. About your enrolling in September."

"Could I not look for a job?"

"What job, for God's sake! You need your education to get anywhere."

"But it's different down here. I'd probably have to start again in First Year – "

"Nonsense. That's why we're seeing this man – to see how and where he can fit you in."

"What about James?"

"I didn't think you'd be that worried about him! We'll work something out. Rosaleen is enquiring about a day-centre that takes special children. Even if that doesn't work out, I'll bring him with me to work, if needs be. You need your schooling, Rossa. You've lost enough ground already."

He lay awake for a long time that night contemplating his future. The prospect did not please him. He could see them, teasing him on the bus, mocking his accent in class, sniggering at how he towered above the other First Years. There would be Margie, of course, but she would be two to three years ahead of him. And there would be teachers. Teachers were often the worst.

"Well that might be the way they do it in Her Majesty's

schools, Mr Fox, but it's not the way we do it down here
. . ."

"Fold your arms, boys, and pay attention. In your case,
Foxie, fold your Armalite . . ."

He turned to face the wall. The patterned wallpaper
dissolved into bold newsprint.

Liverpool Snatch Boy-Wonder Keeper

*Liverpool FC today signed up fifteen-year-old keeper
Rossa Fox from the little-known Irish club Portabeg
United. Fox had come to the attention of Liverpool
scouts after a series of rave notices in the local press,
particularly his feat of saving THREE penalties in a
Junior Cup match. Rossa said he was thrilled to be
joining his favourite team. His mother, Maureen, said
she was anxious about the move at first but Liverpool
had been very reassuring. "They have promised to look
after his schooling – and the financial side is very
attractive," said the petite brunette (35) who is
separated and has one other child. "I'm very proud of
Rossa," she added. And Liverpool supremo, Bill
Shankly's comment? "From what my scouts have told
me, Ray Clemence had better look out!" said the genial
Scot . . .*

Chapter Eighteen

The tension was palpable as the Portabeg community filed into the hall of Liscrone School. Margie's comment about the meeting being "troublesome" had been borne out by rumours that had swept through the parish about "a deal being done".

Michael Nelson sat at the table at the top of the hall, busily leafing through a bulky file of documents. The three other committee members looked out over the crowd at nobody in particular. Each of them in turn seemed unsure of what to do with his hands. One latticed and unlatticed his fingers, another repeatedly slicked back his hair with both hands, while the third sat on his hands for long periods. The din reached a crescendo. Michael Nelson finally stood up to speak.

"All right, ladies and gentlemen. It's time we got going. The committee had an exhaustive – and exhausting! – meeting with the County Council yesterday, in which we discussed all aspects of the proposed dump and the ongoing protest. The Council stressed that, at all times, as a local authority, they attempt to accommodate the wishes of local communities, insofar as that is possible – "

"Rubbish!" a voice interrupted.

"If it is, don't dump it here!" a second voice chortled.

Michael Nelson ignored both interventions.

"– equally, as a local authority, they are committed to meeting the needs of the communities they serve. One of those needs is refuse disposal and that is now at a critical state, as other landfill sites are full, with one exception. Hence the urgent need for a new site – "

"Not at Portabeg, thank you!" came the retort of Mary Roarty, who still carried the obvious scars of her battle with the earth-mover.

"Good on you, Mary!"

"As previously stated," Michael Nelson continued with patent growing impatience, "the Council has carried out a thorough examination of all available sites, employing the latest technology in geological, hydrographical and other tests – "

"Don't mind the big words, what's their final decision?"

"I'm coming to that," Michael Nelson replied wearily. "Having done so and having listened to the objections outlined at various stages of the planning process, the Council still believes that Portabeg remains the best possible option as a landfill site – "

There was uproar as a concerted howl of protest surged from the floor, accompanied by loud stamping of feet. Michael Nelson waited patiently for the tumult to subside. When the whistles and catcalls finally ended, he resumed.

"I wish to make it clear that I am simply relaying the views of the Council thus far. They are not my views, nor those of the committee. However, in the light of the recent disturbance, the Council has had a re-think on the entrance to the proposed site and it now proposes to open a new entrance on Council land, one mile back from Portabeg on the Drumroe road, at a point which is 800 yards from the nearest house. Further, on the actual site, the Council proposes to plant an additional screen of two-hundred evergreen trees and also to implement a new cell structure in the actual dump which would help considerably in containing the refuse and preventing pollution."

"What about Lissy?" a voice called from the back of the hall. Rossa was relieved to hear that someone had remembered her.

"In respect of Lissy, the Council, while recognising the fact that, in law, she has no title to the premises she now occupies – nevertheless, as a mark of good faith, the council are prepared to offer her a parcel of rough grazing on land they hold at Moneen on the other side of the bog and, further, to construct a 'tigeen' for her on that land. This offer has been communicated to Lissy and I understand she is prepared to accept it."

He paused to take a drink from a glass of water.

"I'm nearly finished," he said with a weak smile.

"So are we all," came the reply.

"Based on all the foregoing, the committee have considered the situation and have reluctantly agreed with the Council and have accepted these new terms – "

Uproar again drowned his words and angry cries of "Sell-out!" "Cowards!" and "No way!" rent the air. He waited for a slight lull in the protest before adding his final words:

" – having been empowered by the community to negotiate on their behalf. Thank you!"

He sat down, took a long drink of water and buried his head in his hands while the protest continued. When it finally subsided enough to allow Mary Roarty to lead the opposition to the agreement, "The Battery" Lynch beat her to it.

"Hurl them, Portabeg! Come on the beggars!" His words eased the tension somewhat, as laughter rippled through the hall.

"Thank you, Mr Lynch," Mary Roarty began. "Indeed you have summed our position up. We *didn't* hurl them! We lay down and let them walk on us, or rather, drive over us!" She indicated one arm in a sling with another that was heavily bandaged – a gesture that brought loud cheers and applause from the audience. "We are indeed reduced to beggars looking for crumbs of consolation from the Council's table. This is a total sell-out and certainly not what I got myself mangled and nearly killed for. When all is said and done, it's still a dump, despite all the fancy language." She hobbled off the platform to a huge ovation.

A succession of speakers followed, most of the words in similar vein to Mary's, but a number of them pleaded for understanding for the committee who had "a difficult job to do".

Fr O'Mahony spoke last asking for understanding on both sides, expressing the wish that – whatever the outcome – the community would stand together.

Michael Nelson stood once more to respond to the speakers.

"I have just four things to say. We as a committee had a tough job on our hands and we did our best.

"One – we succeeded in moving the problem of the heavy traffic away from Portabeg.

"Two – we got additional screening for the dump and the most modern methods of infill.

"Three – we fought Lissy's case and won her a reasonable outcome.

"Four – of course it's still a dump, but the bottom line is that, in law, we have no option but to accept it. The Council have played this by the rules all the way and, in plain words, they beat us hands down."

His words brought ripples of applause from the audience as the meeting concluded. But as the crowd drifted out into the night, the animated conversation, argument and counter-argument underlined the fact that while the Dump War was lost, there were many battles still to be fought.

Portabeg was a divided community.

They picked their way across the bog, hopping from one tuft of spongy moss to another. Now that the bog was drying out, it was a more exciting way to get to Lissy's than by staying on the rough gravelled road. The only problem was James, who had developed a pattern of jumping in the opposite direction at regular intervals.

"Come on, James!" Rossa called in exasperation. "Two steps forward, one step back. It'll take us all day at this rate."

"He's getting there," Margie said. "I don't think you'll change him out of his routine, judging by that look on his face."

"No way!"

Rossa had been anxious to see Lissy since he had heard of the "arrangement" that was outlined at the meeting the previous evening. He had not been totally convinced by Mr Nelson's claim that she was prepared to accept the Council's offer.

Having Margie accompany him to Lissy's was an unexpected surprise.

"Daddy announced he was going to Dublin this morning. Said something had come up at head office. I think it was more to do with last night's meeting. Mary Roarty really annoyed him."

Rossa could sense the relief in Margie's voice, whatever the reason for his abrupt departure.

James suddenly became very excited, pointing to the sky behind them. A helicopter swooped in over their heads, quite low, and then disappeared behind Scroogawn.

"Must be the Council moving in on Lissy already," Margie joked.

Rossa remained silent, tracing the path of the helicopter across the skyline. Move on, he whispered to himself. Move on.

"Pardon?" Margie sensed his unease, but the attention of both was diverted by James toppling off a tuft in his excitement and slithering into black ooze up to his ankles. He began to scream.

"I'm in trouble now," Rossa sighed. "Mum will murder me!"

"Shoes off! Shoes off!" James shouted.

"All right! All right!" Rossa replied angrily, propping his brother on a bed of heather and removing his soaking shoes and socks. He offered them to Margie.

"Could you take these? I'll carry this fellow the rest of the way."

He lifted James, slung him over his shoulder, and headed towards Lissy's.

A robust burst of song greeted them.

"Johnny, lovely Johnny
Do you mind the day
You came to my window
To lead me away . . ."

Lissy was in the paddock milking Tosca. Pinkerton, lying on top of the paddock wall, gave a bark of recognition and jumped down to greet the visitors.

"Ye're welcome. 'Tis nice to have friendly faces about the place!"

She took the tin can from underneath Tosca, whispered, *"Grazie! Grazie!"* to the goat, stood up and arched her back. "There's a great stiffness in my bones! The years are upon me."

"Have you had many visitors, Lissy?" Rossa asked, propping James up on the wall.

"Don't be talking! 'Tis like I was the Queen of England, with men in shiny cars and fine suits coming to pay court to me. And all they want is for me to move out of here!"

"What do you think of moving?" Margie asked.

"'Tis not what I want, but I have little say in the end of all. They tell me I have no claim on this place and they will build me a proper house over at Moneen. A proper house! I ask you! Isn't this little place proper enough . . . ? Proper enough."

She sang a snatch of a song.

"Addio, fiorito asil . . .

Farewell, flowery refuge . . ."

Rossa surveyed the tumbledown cottage with its rusting roof, chimney askew and broken windows. Flowery it was not, but a refuge it was – for Lissy. More than a refuge. A home. He knew from her prolonged sigh that it was saddening her greatly to leave this place.

"I told them I'd stay here. The dump wouldn't bother me. But no, they said. They needed a place to turn their big lorries and this was it. They're going to flatten it next week – "

"Flatten it?"

"Flatten it indeed! With their big bulldozers."

"But they can't!" Rossa could not believe what he was hearing. "You have no house – "

"They're giving me a caravan over at Moneen while the houseen is being built. There's a big lorry coming on Saturday to move all the bits and pieces – including my family." She ruffled the coat of Butterfly who had curled up at her feet.

Rossa and Margie exchanged anxious glances. Things were happening at a bewildering speed.

"Chore! Chore! Chore!" James interrupted their thoughts abruptly.

"He wants to see the *uainín*!" Lissy said in a brighter voice. "Come in, let ye!" She noticed James's bare feet. "Was it paddling in the river you were, *a stór*?"

"He fell down in the bog," Rossa explained.

"What matter," Lissy led them towards the house. "'Tis good clean dirt."

As they entered the house, they were collectively brought to a halt by two sharp reports that echoed across the bog.

"Someone shooting the poor little rabbits again," Lissy said.

Rossa felt a strange chill run through his body. He hoped she was right.

A plaintive cry greeted them when they moved inside. The tiny lamb came trotting unsteadily towards Lissy.

"There's the boy that's growing big and strong!" Lissy said as the lamb nudged his nose against her boots. "He's got to be a right *peata*! I don't know what I'll do with you at all!" She lifted up the spindly body and placed it in James's already outstretched arms. All three visitors marvelled at the lamb's progress, but James especially was entranced by the warm woolly body that lay in his arms.

Lissy went through her ritual of selecting one of her records, carefully removing it from the sleeve, placing it on the turntable and winding up the gramophone before gently dropping the needle onto the record. The song was now familiar to Rossa and Margie.

"One fine day we'll see

A wisp of smoke rising

from the distant horizon of the sea."

Lissy sang with the crackling record until she suddenly remembered something.

"Amn't I the forgetful one? Not offering my visitors anything!" She prised open a battered biscuit tin and withdrew three packets of crisps which she distributed among the visitors. She resumed singing.

"What will he say? What will he say?

He will call 'Butterfly' from the distance."

Rossa could not shake off the uneasy feeling that had remained with him since he had heard the shots. Outside,

Pinkerton too was uneasy, emitting low growls as he sat stiffly on his haunches, ears pricked. The growls became shrill barks. Rossa peered through the broken window. A figure came half-tumbling, half-slithering down Scroogawn. Rossa's throat felt raw and parched. He could hear voices now. Two figures appeared at the top of Scroogawn. The lone figure reached level ground and began running in a crazy weaving pattern. Pinkerton stood alert now, barking furiously. Rossa felt beads of sweat break out on his brow. The lone figure was heading directly towards Lissy's house, his long hair flailing in the air. Pinkerton crouched, ready to spring. The man glanced quickly backwards, then made a renewed lunge forward, screaming wildly at the dog.

The dog sprang. There was a loud crack. The dog contorted wildly in mid-air before falling awkwardly to the ground where he lay motionless. Rossa watched in horror, now joined by Margie and Lissy. He stood transfixed and realised too late what he should do. He brushed past Margie to the door and fumbled furiously for a bolt that would lock it.

He was sent hurtling backwards as the door burst open and the wild unkempt figure charged into the kitchen, brandishing a gun. There were screams of terror from the occupants within. Rossa crashed against the legs of a chair and spun around to face the invader. For the second time in a few days, he had come face-to-face with his father.

Chapter Nineteen

"Into the corner – all of youse," he barked. "Jesus – you!" he shrieked on recognising his son. "Move!" He gestured towards the corner, waving the gun wildly. Rossa crawled to where Margie and Lissie cowered in the corner. Where was James?

His father turned to the window.

"OK," he shouted, fighting to regain his breath. "Let's take it easy. There's a woman and children in here. We don't want anyone gettin' hurt, do we?"

"OK! OK!" came the reply from outside.

Patrick Fox threw his head back against the wall and slid slowly down into a hunched position, breathing deeply.

"You – shot – Pinkerton!" Rossa fought to control his feelings.

"Pinkerton? What's Pinkerton?"

"The dog, Lissy's dog. You shot him."

"The bastard was going for me. What did you want me to do? Stop and say, 'Nice doggy, do you mind if I pass?' I'm sorry, missus, but . . ."

"That's your only answer, isn't it?" As the shock began to subside, Rossa's anger was mounting. "If someone gets in your way, take him out. That's your only answer."

"Listen, sunshine. I don't need lectures from you or anyone – what's that godawful racket?"

It was only when the mayhem had abated that they became aware of the record playing incongruously in the background to Patrick Fox's left.

"Are we in the middle of a concert here, or what?"

He lashed at the gramophone with the barrel of the gun. There was a resounding crack as the record split and the needle jammed between the broken segments. Rossa looked in horror to Lissy. She leaned against a chair, her face drained of colour, silently mouthing words which Rossa could not discern. He was livid.

"You bastard! There was no need for that – "

"Hey now, that's no way to talk to your father!" He glanced through the window, peering to the left and right. "As you can see, I'm in a spot of bother here, no doubt thanks to you, squealer – "

"I didn't squeal on you." Rossa was aware of Margie watching him in total bewilderment.

"Well, who else knew, sunshine? I wasn't exactly leaving my calling cards around the place, you must – "

His words were drowned by the deafening whirr of the helicopter which came in over Scroogawn and swooped over the house. It circled the house several times before falling away towards Portabeg. Rossa watched his father intently as his darting eyes attempted to follow the helicopter's path. There was desperation in those eyes, a desperation that frightened Rossa. He looked anxiously about the darkened room. Where was James?

The helicopter provided the answer. There was a billowing of the oilcloth that covered the table. Something began to emerge from beneath the table.

"Jesus!" Patrick Fox was startled by this unexpected move and aimed his pistol at the bulging oilcloth.

"No!" Rossa screamed as he dived towards the table. The tiny head of the lamb appeared, looking uncertainly about before trotting over to Lissy. There was no further movement beneath the oilcloth.

"It's – only – Lissy's pet lamb!" he blurted. "There's no need to shoot it."

"Right little menagerie we have here!" his father commented cynically. "Are you not going to introduce your friends to your father, or are you too ashamed?"

"This is Lissy. This is her house. And this is Margie."

"The girlfriend, what? I'm thinkin' you're a bit of a lad all right, Rossa. Haysheds, remote cottages – a bit of a lad – "

"This is my father," Rossa interrupted in little more than a whisper. "He escaped from prison. He plants bombs, shoots dogs and breaks records."

"My, but we're the angry young man today," his father replied. "There's hope for us yet!"

"Fox. Patrick Fox!" a voice called over a tinny megaphone from the paddock.

"Anseo!" came the reply.

"You might as well give up now. There's no way out of here. You are totally surrounded. So just throw out your gun and come out slowly with your hands on your head!"

There was no response from within.

"Fox. Patrick Fox!" the voice resumed.

"Yeh! Yeh! I hear you. Just shut up a while. I'm trying to think."

Patrick Fox surveyed the scene before him. An agitated old woman seated on a chair cradling a lamb, a young girl fidgeting nervously by her side and a young boy, his son, staring defiantly at him. He gave a nervous laugh.

"There's no doubt! Of all the bars in all the world, I had to walk into this one!"

"You might as well do what they say, Dad," Rossa said. A succession of wailing sirens could be heard in the direction of Portabeg, rising to a crescendo as the garda cars sped up the bog road. "They're all over the place."

He felt sorry for his father now. He had the look of a trapped animal, eyes darting to the right and left, desperately looking for a way out of his predicament.

"I'm not done yet!" his father panted. "Just let me think! I'm not going back to that bloody Kesh . . ."

Lissy spoke for the first time since the intruder had invaded her house.

"'Tis a fearful thing when all are against you. You have no one to turn to but yourself."

The house was now enveloped in a cacophony of sirens.

"The helicopter!" Patrick Fox cried. "That's it! I'll demand the helicopter to get me out – with one of youse as hostage!"

"And when yourself won't answer yourself," Lissy continued, "'tis the most fearful thing of all."

"Come on, Dad," Rossa said. "That only happens in the movies and even then, it doesn't work."

He watched with growing anxiety as his father kept switching the gun from hand to hand, each time wiping the sweaty palm of the free hand on his jumper.

"I'm not going back there," Patrick Fox whispered. "Or if I do," – he paused to stare at the gun in his hand – "I'll be in a box."

"Don't be stupid, Dad," Rossa cried.

The megaphone voice was barely audible above the sirens.

"What about it, Fox? You've had time to think. Do the sensible thing!"

"'Don't be stupid!' 'Do the sensible thing!'" Patrick Fox hissed. "Youse are all full of advice, aren't you? Do the sensible thing! Walk back into a hellhole for twenty years! Oh it's very easy to do the sensible thing all right! I might as well – "

A loud sneeze from beneath the table interrupted him. Rossa froze as his father pointed the gun at the billowing oilcloth and moved away from the window in a wide arc, keeping his eyes fixed on the table.

"Jesus!" he whispered, "this place is full of surprises!" He straightened his arm and focused his aim along the barrel of the gun.

"No, Dad, no!" Rossa shrieked. He leaped forward to the table. "It's only – James." He lifted up the oilcloth slowly to reveal his brother curled up beside Siegfried. James held his hands tightly over his eyes.

"James? The wee fellow?" Patrick Fox lowered his gun and sank back on a rickety chair by the fire. Rossa nodded and bent down to his brother.

"Come on out, James, Daddy is here!"

The boy's response was to shudder and burrow his body further behind Siegfried.

Patrick Fox laid his gun down on the hearth.

"Come on, wee fellow!" his voice quivered, "I'll not harm you."

Siegfried uttered a low growl. Lissy moved from her chair and knelt at the table.

"Come on, *a stór*." She reached in and laid her hand gently on the boy's head. *"Chore! Chore! Chore!"* she whispered *"Chore! Chore! Chore!"*

Slowly the boy dropped his hands, clambered over Siegfried's body and crawled out to take Lissy's hand. He kept his head bowed and stared at the floor as he began to rock his body to and fro.

"Jesus!" Patrick Fox slid to his knees and extended his arms towards James. Very slowly he enveloped the tiny body of his younger son in his embrace and drew the boy towards him. Lissy let James's hand go. The boy's arms hung by his side. He showed no response to his father's embrace. Patrick Fox's body heaved as he began to sob loudly. Rossa reached forwards to grasp his father's hand. He could not remember when he had last touched his father.

The bolt shot back and the cottage door creaked open. The gardaí and soldiers crouched behind their cover points, weapons held ready, prepared to pounce on their quarry.

Rossa stepped out into the sunlight, shielding his eyes from the unaccustomed glare. He couldn't see anybody, but felt a threatening presence all about him.

"He's coming out!" His voice was little more than a croak. "It's all right, he isn't armed."

Patrick Fox emerged unsteadily into the light.

167

"Hands above your head, Fox. Hands above your head!" a voice roared from beyond the paddock wall.

"He isn't armed," Rossa repeated. "Don't harm him!"

"Hands above your head!" the voice roared even louder. Patrick Fox lifted his hands in a daze. As soon as he had moved a few paces away from the door, mayhem broke out. Uniformed bodies swept past Rossa in a blur. His father was crash-tackled to the ground as a number of bodies dived in on top of him.

"Don't hurt him!" Rossa shrieked in terror. "He can't – "

Rossa himself was bundled roughly away from the house and tumbled over the wall. He heard his father give a cry of pain as his arms were pinioned roughly behind his back by one man while another quickly searched his body for weapons. Two guards rushed into the house. Rossa cried out again but his words were drowned in the confusion.

It was all over in a couple of minutes. His father, handcuffed behind his back, was bundled into the back seat of a dark blue car which reversed noisily and then sped away down the gravel track, followed by the two squad cars. Rossa's last view of his father was of a hunched figure bent forward until his head rested on the seat in front of him, his long black hair totally covering his face.

Chapter Twenty

Sergeant Fogarty took them home in the squad car. James held his hands over his eyes for the entire journey. Rossa and Margie were still dazed by the rapidity of the events of the previous hour. They had been unwilling to leave Lissy but she insisted that she was all right. As Rossa left he noticed her place the segments of the broken "One Fine Day" record carefully back in the sleeve as if nothing had happened to it . . .

"What will happen to my father?" he asked Sergeant Fogarty.

"He's on his way to Limerick prison," the sergeant replied. "They'll have to organise extradition over the border." He negotiated a broken stretch of the road cautiously. "He was a foolish man to come down here. The Special Branch were all over the place."

"It was a pure fluke he came here. He didn't know we were here."

"Is that a fact? That was unlucky, so."

Yeh, unlucky. His father had always been unlucky. He turned to Margie. She gave him a reassuring smile and slid her hand across his. It was a nice feeling.

Maureen Fox came running down the driveway. She swept James into her arms.

"Mother of God!" she cried. "Are you all right? I heard all the racket. What happened? Why are you – it was your father, wasn't it?"

"Calm down Mum," Rossa said, somewhat embarrassed in front of Margie. "It's all over."

"What's all over? Nobody will tell me anything – "

"Your husband has been recaptured," Sergeant Fogarty explained. "It all ended peacefully. Nobody was hurt." Except Lissy, Rossa thought. The images of Pinkerton's twisted bleeding body and of the shattered record flashed across his mind.

"But how? Where?" his mother persisted.

"Your son will tell you all, Mrs Fox. He was in the thick of it," Sergeant Fogarty explained. "Now if you don't mind, I have to leave this lassie home and catch up with my work." He drove off quickly before either Rossa could speak to Margie or his mother could ask another question.

Rossa related the story of his two meetings with his father with considerable difficulty. His mother constantly interrupted him with questions and reprimands.

"But why did you not tell me? . . ."

"You should never have gone to Lissy's while he was at large – "

"I never knew about the hayshed, you're supposed to tell me where you are going . . ."

"I can't believe he arrived here by accident – "

Rossa left out some details, particularly the shooting of Pinkerton. She would go completely hysterical if she knew about that.

"It was James that made him surrender," he said. "When he saw him, he just sort of collapsed."

His mother lit a cigarette.

"He collapsed too when – we found out – about James," she said quietly. "Couldn't take it! Especially when James wouldn't respond. He blames it on everyone. Me. The Orangemen that delivered him in the hospital, as he put it. It changed him totally. He became moody, angry. He used to frighten me. I often wonder would he have got – involved like he did if . . . And then Sophie. That finished him. What's the point in wondering?" she sighed. "It's all different now."

A muffled sound came from the corner of the room.

"Look at you!" She threw her arms up in a gesture of helplessness. James had returned to the shelter of his bin. "A whole week he had gone without the bin. I thought I had him cured of it. A whole week . . ."

Jim and Rosaleen Daly arrived as soon as they heard the news of Patrick Fox's arrest. Rossa had to endure re-telling the story and his mother's reprimands. At least I'm spared my cousins' comments, he thought.

The door of the mobile home was flung open and Paula and Majella burst in.

"Have you two no manners?" their father snapped. Paula ignored him.

"Have ye heard the news?" she asked.

"We were just hearing about your uncle's arrest when you two – "

"No, not that!" Paula's smirk stretched from ear to ear.

"Well what?" Their father's annoyance was growing.

"You tell them, Jelly," Paula said.

"No, you said you wanted to," Majella replied.

"No, Jelly, you – "

"God, you two will be the death of me," Jim Daly cut in, clearly exasperated. "If you have news that's important, would one of you tell us – now?"

Paula threw a sour glance at her father and then beamed with delight as she directed all her attention at Rossa.

"The Nelsons are leaving," she crowed. "There's a big For Sale sign outside their house!"

They were standing outside the record shop, the three of them, pointing to a particular record. The beautiful dark-eyed assistant with the long flowing hair smiled and held up a record. No. No. The next one. She held up another record. Yes , that's the one. They could read the title on the cardboard sleeve. One Fine Day.

The woman in the window began to sing. Rossa looked to his right. Margie and James were laughing. Then the blinding flash. The woman disappeared. The record broke into three huge segments which sliced through the window and came hurtling towards them. No

– o – o – o –

He sat upright in a cold sweat. There was a strange glow all around him. Was it a nightmare or reality? He looked around, half afraid of what he might see . . .

The glow came from the television which was still on long after closedown. He shivered as he climbed out of bed to switch it off and retreated again into the dark.

There was no sign of Margie next day. She did not attend school, but Paula's news was correct. Rossa ventured as far as the bend in the road. From there, at a distance of a half a mile, he could see the For Sale sign.

"They're supposed to be moving to Dublin," Majella said.

"Australia, I heard," Paula added. "No loss either." She sensed that Rossa was about to vent his anger on her. "He sold us out over the dump and now he's selling out himself," she added quickly.

Rossa moped around the garden next morning. He had to see Margie. To find out. Why? When? He chipped the ball up and began juggling. If the Nelsons were leaving, so was he.

Kennedy receives from Heighway, holds it, looks up –

He wasn't going to be left with two giddybiddy cousins for company –

Kennedy tries a snap shot. Oh my goodness, He'll want to forget that one. Not having one of his better days.

As he bent to retrieve the ball from the ditch, Rossa noticed a car speeding past in the direction of Liscrone. He recognised the figure of Michael Nelson hunched over the steering wheel.

Rossa lobbed the ball towards the door of the mobile home. "Come on, James," he called. "We're going for a walk."

"Rocky! Rocky! Rocky!" James replied. He was kneeling on the pathway watching the terrapin's slow progress through the long grass.

"Yeh! Rocky can come too. Put him on a lead! Come on! We haven't much time."

He might as well have put Rocky on a lead, so slow was their progress. James carried Rocky in a plastic box and stopped every few yards to rearrange Rocky's bed of grass in the box.

When they eventually reached the Nelsons' house,

Rossa became extremely nervous. What if Margie wasn't there? He knew she wasn't at school. He had watched the road all morning. What if her father returned as quickly as he had left? He glanced at the For Sale sign. "Luxury two-storey residence. View by appointment" . . . He had no appointment but he wasn't turning back now.

The door opened slightly.

"Yes?" He had only caught an occasional glimpse of Margie's mother before now. Usually in the car or in a distant pew in church. You would never meet her in Lovely's or see her at a protest meeting.

"The Reverend Mother never leaves the convent," Paula had said. Rossa was taken aback on meeting her face-to-face. Her slight figure was neatly dressed but her gaunt features and greying hair disquieted him. She looked – old, almost as if she were Margie's grandmother.

"Yes?"

"Sorry. I'm Rossa. I'm a friend of Margie's . . ."

"I recognise you all right." Her tone was extremely cautious.

"I heard she wasn't at school. I just wondered if she was sick – or something – "

"No. She's not sick. She – just had to help her father with some work. He's – under a lot of pressure." The tone was defensive now.

"Could I see her – for a few minutes?"

Mrs Nelson looked anxiously around to a grandfather clock in the corner of the hall.

"I don't know," she said. "Wait there!"

Is it such a big deal? Rossa thought. James had released Rocky onto the gravelled area.

"Watch him now, James! If he gets lost here we'll never – "

"Hi!" Margie's quiet voice caught him unawares.

"Just a few minutes," her mother called from behind her. "Daddy will be back soon."

"Yes, Mum."

They strolled across the gravel.

"What are you doing here? You know –"

"I just wanted to know how you were. I saw your father go down the road. It's not a crime, is it?"

She ignored his last remark.

"He's gone to Ennis. He won't be long. He drives very fast."

"I know. So, did he find out about what happened at Lissy's?"

"He knows about your father being captured – but not about me being there. Mum didn't say anything."

"Good for her. She – doesn't say much, does she?"

There was no reply. Change the subject, change the subject.

"What's with this?" he gestured towards the For Sale sign.

She shrugged her shoulders.

"Daddy says his head-office wants him based in Dublin. So . . ."

"What do you think?"

"I don't really want to move."

"And your mum?"

"She's – not too keen either."

"Could he not stay in Dublin – for a few days a week?" He knew such an arrangement would suit them both, if not her father.

175

"When Daddy decides, that's it."

"When will you move?"

"Won't be for a while. We have to sell the house first."

"I'll miss you."

"Thanks. The same goes for me."

Rossa took a deep breath.

"In fact, if you're not going to be – "

James interrupted him at the crucial moment.

"Rocky gone! Rocky gone! Rocky gone!"

"Christmas!" Rossa cried in exasperation. "I told you to watch him, James."

The three spent the next five minutes crawling around the gravel in search of the terrapin.

Mrs Nelson appeared at the door.

"It's time, Margie," she said.

"Just a minute, Mum. James has lost his terrapin – "

"Daddy will be here – "

"I know. I know. I'm coming!"

I could cheerfully murder you, James, Rossa thought. If Mr Nelson comes back now, I'm for it. He suddenly remembered being with his father in the hayloft.

"If we all stay very quiet for a minute and listen," he suggested.

They spread out and listened. Margie heard the tiniest scraping noise and saw a pebble move.

"There!" she cried triumphantly. Rossa pounced and popped Rocky into his box.

"Come on, James!" He turned to Margie. "Lissy is moving on Saturday. Will you be there?"

"Don't know. Depends – "

Rossa was relieved to get back home before Michael Nelson returned. His relief was to be short-lived.

A loud persistent knocking on the door at eight-thirty the following morning irritated Maureen Fox.

"What in God's name has got into Jim this morning? James, where's your other sock? Rossa, would you ever tell Jim to keep his hair on – I'm going as fast as I can!"

Rossa rubbed the sleep from his eyes and unbolted the door. He leaped backwards when he found himself confronted by a very angry Michael Nelson.

"Come out here, you young pup! Come out here and I'll teach you a lesson before you're sent back to the slums of Belfast where you belong!"

His bulging eyes and shaking frame terrified Rossa into silence. He grabbed Rossa's arm roughly. Rossa reacted by holding on to the door with his free hand. As the initial shock subsided, he found his voice.

"Leave off. You friggin' madman!"

His mother came running to her son's aid.

"What's going on? Leave him alone!" she shouted at Michael Nelson.

"Leave him alone? Why doesn't he leave people alone? I knew from the day you lot moved here there'd be trouble. You know nothing else!"

Maureen Fox was also incensed.

"Now wait a minute! Just who do you think you are, and what kind of accusations are you making about my son?"

Before Michael Nelson could answer, Jim Daly arrived, followed by his daughters.

"What's going on?" he asked calmly.

"That's what I would like to know," Maureen added, struggling to control her temper.

"I'll tell you what's going on!" Michael Nelson bellowed.

"By all means, Michael," Jim Daly said. "But there's no need to tell the whole parish – and I think you could let the lad go. He's not going to make a run for it!"

Rossa's arm was grudgingly released. He could hear the sniggers of his cousins behind his father.

"All right," Michael Nelson continued. "I went out this morning to find slogans daubed along my front wall." He continued to stare at Rossa.

"And what brought you down here?" Jim asked.

"Very simple. The trail!"

"The trail?"

"Yes, this fellow is about as clumsy as his father – "

"There's no need for that," Jim Daly interrupted him.

"There's every need!" Michael Nelson's accusation was growing more and more triumphant. "He was in such a hurry away from his dirty work that he left a trail of yellow paint behind him, right to the end of the mobile home – to there!"

He pointed to an empty paint can with a brush protruding from it, nestling in the bottom of the ditch.

Rossa stared at the paint can, incredulous.

"I'd hardly be that stupid," he said.

"Panic can cause stupidity," Michael Nelson remarked dryly.

Maureen Fox turned to her son.

"Rossa did you – ?"

"Of course not, Mum!" He couldn't believe his mother would even think he might be responsible for the slogan writing.

"This is obviously a job for the guards," Jim Daly suggested.

"Indeed it is!" Michael Nelson agreed. "I've already rung them. Sergeant Fogarty is probably at my house by now!"

"Well, let's go and inspect the damage then," Jim Daly said. "I'll take Rossa up," he whispered to his sister-in-law. "There's no need – "

"There's every need! If my son is being accused of something, I want to see what it is."

Jim turned to his daughters.

"Get along, you two, you'll be late for the school bus!"

"But Dad," Paula pleaded, barely concealing her delight at Rossa's predicament. "We want to see the scene of the crime!"

"Go!" her father snapped. The sisters trooped reluctantly back to their house.

"We'll visit you in jail, Rossa, won't we, Jelly?" Paula called before shutting the door on her father's reaction.

Sergeant Fogarty was pacing up and down the road, studying the scene, when the others arrived.

"Messy business," he said on greeting Michael Nelson.

Daubed crudely in large letters of bright yellow paint along the length of the roadside wall were the words:

TRAITER SELLS OUT

"Messy indeed," Michael Nelson agreed. "Except that we have the culprit for you!" He pointed an accusing finger at Rossa.

"How so?"

Michael Nelson triumphantly related the evidence of the paint-trail leading to the discarded paint can.

"It's cut and dried," he concluded.

"And what has this young man to say?" Sergeant Fogarty turned to Rossa.

"I had nothing to do with it," Rossa said. "At least I know how to spell 'traitor'," he added.

"Hah! The oldest trick in the book," Michael Nelson jibed. "Spell it wrong to throw them off the track."

"Rossa was at home all night," Maureen Fox countered.

"How do you know?" Michael Nelson asked.

"Because I don't sleep very well, Mr Nelson – and I'd hear him going out. That's if he had any reason to go out."

"He had reason a plenty – "

"Now, if ye don't mind," Sergeant Fogarty intervened, "I will conduct this investigation."

There was an embarrassing silence until Sergeant Fogarty spoke again.

"Now I'll make some notes, examine this mysterious paint-trail and take your statements. I presume no one will be leaving the jurisdiction?" he added with a raised eyebrow. He patted his breast pocket. "Dammit! I came without my notebook. Would you have a few sheets of notepaper, Michael?"

"Of course!" Michael Nelson hurried into the house. As he did so, Rossa caught a glimpse of Margie at an upper window. He shrugged his shoulders in a gesture of helplessness. He hoped she understood.

Michael Nelson returned with a sheaf of notepaper.

"Begor, I hope I won't need all that!" Sergeant Fogarty joked. "Now I suggest you all go your separate ways and leave me to do my job."

"The whole thing is crazy," Rossa said in the car on the way back. "He's just picking on me because he doesn't like me."

"But what about the paint-trail?" his mother enquired.

"Someone is trying to set me up."

"Who?"

"Don't know. Wish I did! I wouldn't mind giving JJ a spelling test, though."

Chapter Twenty-One

Lissy stood, hand on hips, surveying the crazily-stacked jumble that represented her belongings: tables, odd chairs, a broken sofa, a bed, an assortment of pots and utensils, boxes of crockery, buckets and basins. The gramophone and record chest stood apart from the pile, the morning sun playing on their fine-grained wood.

"We did a good morning's work," she said to Rossa, "even if all these bits and pieces don't amount to much of a *carn* in the end of all."

"They're your bits and pieces," Rossa replied. It had been both a satisfying and a poignant experience to help Lissy clear her house. He was glad to have been able to help her but he was aware that, for all its broken-down appearance, its leaking roof and crumbling walls, this place had been Lissy's home for many years. Her frequent deep sighs as they worked betrayed her emotions. Her sadness had been lifted by Rossa's finding a strange book which had slipped down behind the dresser.

"Le mie canzoni!" Lissy cried excitedly as she lifted its

faded and frayed leather cover and turned its well-thumbed leaves. "It's my songbook – my father's songbook! All his songs are here!" She hummed various airs as she turned the pages. "I thought 'twas long gone!" She closed the book and clasped it to her breast for a long time.

Their silent reflection was broken by a loud commotion from the paddock. Two council workers were trying to coax Tosca up a ramp and into a crate in the back of a lorry. Having defied their best efforts, Tosca's patience was now wearing thin and she advanced menacingly towards one of the men. The man vaulted the paddock wall, swearing loudly. Lissy laughed heartily at Tosca's antics.

She entered the paddock and began to sing softly as she approached Tosca.

"Love and music, these have I lived for,

Nor ever harmed a living being . . ."

She turned and walked up the ramp. The goat trotted meekly behind.

"I've seen it all now, singing to a goat!" the man in the corner of the paddock chortled.

"Doesn't it work?" His companion who had leapt the wall said as he watched Lissy close the crate.

"Why wouldn't it work?" she called out. "Isn't that Tosca's own song?" She broke into song once more.

"Love and music, these have I lived for,

Nor ever harmed a living being . . ."

The lorry bounced along the buckled road that led to Lissy's new home at Moneen. The journey was short – no more than a couple of miles. Rossa was glad of this, as he sat hunched in the back of the lorry with Siegfried cradled in his lap. Across from him, Lissy stroked Butterfly's head and sang gently to her. Three cardboard boxes lay between them. Strange mewling sounds came from the boxes as Carmen, Figaro and Violetta protested at their incarceration. At the other end of the lorry, hidden from Rossa by the swaying pile of furniture, Tosca bleated her discomfort and tested the strength of the crate with an occasional butt.

"At least Pinkerton will be happy," Lissy said, looking back at her tumble-down home. "He won't have to move from his bed at the foot of Scroogawn."

Rossa dreaded this moment. Pinkerton had not been mentioned since the day his father had shot the dog.

"I'm sorry – about Pinkerton. My dad panicked – "

"'Tis behind us now. No matter. I'll miss him for the sheep. This lady is too proud and beautiful for work like that!" She ruffled Butterfly's coat. "And the old warrior's days are nearly done!" Siegfried stretched himself across Rossa's lap. "Maybe I'll find a *coileán* somewhere. Anyway I only lost a dog. You lost a father."

"Not forever, I hope," Rossa said.

"No," Lissy agreed. "Not forever."

Not forever. He would visit his father when he got the opportunity. And that opportunity might come sooner rather than later. A plan was evolving in his head, a plan instigated by recent events. The meeting with his father, Margie leaving for Dublin, Michael Nelson's charges against him, the prospect of starting school in a strange place. He would go back to Belfast, stay with Eileen Devlin, go to school and get a part-time job to pay his way. The only problem was his mother. She would explode when she heard his plan, but he would persist . . .

The lorry shuddered to a halt.

"Welcome to your new home, Lissy!" the lorry-driver called as he dropped the tailgate. "Your palace is nearly built!"

Two brick-layers were busy laying the final course of blocks which brought the walls to roof level. A caravan was parked nearby. Lissy and Rossa released the dogs and made their way to the caravan.

"There's not much room in here," Lissy said, surveying the small kitchen, "but 'twill do, I suppose. I'll not be entertaining royalty!"

They began the process of unloading Lissy's furniture. The larger pieces would not fit in the caravan and were stored in an improvised lean-to shed used by the builders. The gramophone was given pride of place in the tiny sitting-room and within minutes of its installation, Lissy was singing along to the strains of Il Trovatore.

"Home to the mountains,
One day returning,
All our old happiness
We shall recover . . ."

The builders paused, bemused, before one of them called out:

"Have you no Rolling Stones? That stuff would put years on you!"

Lissy suddenly became agitated as she searched around the kitchen.

"What's wrong?" Rossa asked.

"The worst thing of all!" Lissy sighed. "There's no fireplace. I'll have to light a fire outside to boil a kettle!"

"No, you won't," Rossa laughed. "Look! There's a small gas cooker here."

"Gas? I'd be afraid of that! Wouldn't it blow up in my face?"

"Not at all," Rossa reassured her. "We have one at home. I'll show you!"

He lit and extinguished one of the rings several times.

"Well isn't that a wonder! I still think I'll light a fire outside."

"No! No!" Rossa pleaded. "You must try it!"

Lissy turned on the gas tentatively and struck a match.

"Santo Dio!" She gave a little leap backward as the flames spurted from the ring.

"See! It's easy," Rossa said. "Now all we need is water!"

The builder had the answer to that.

"We brought a can of water but there's the loveliest spring water down at the end of that field where you've tethered the goat."

Rossa filled a bucket from the spring and brought it back to Lissy.

"Well I declare," Lissy said as the kettle sang on the gas ring. "'Tis nearly like being at home! The old warrior is not happy, though. He can't settle at all!"

Siegfried was padding about restlessly, sensing the strangeness of his new surroundings.

"Give him time," Rossa said as he unpacked the crockery.

"Give us all time," Lissy sighed, looking across the bog to the distant Scroogawn. *"Speriamo bene!"*

Rossa got a lift back to Portabeg with the builders.

"We only work a half-day on Saturday. Have to get home and get cleaned up for the action tonight," the younger one said. The older man, balding and bursting out of his overalls, negotiated his way slowly along the broken road in a van that rattled and shook all over.

"I couldn't take any more of that caterwaulin' music," he said.

"Dead right, Sonny," the younger man said. "I don't know how we'll put up with it for the next few weeks. Maybe I'll bring out my Rolling Stones LP!"

He began his Mick Jagger impersonation.

"I am the little red rooster – "

"Jeez," Sonny shouted. "That's even worse!"

Rossa said nothing but glanced anxiously at his watch. A quarter to two. Only time for a sandwich and then off to soccer practice.

"Begor, you have visitors, young fella," Sonny said. "Kojak has come a-calling."

The squad car was parked outside Jim Daly's house.

Rossa's heart began to thud. Was this more trouble from Michael Nelson?

"Thanks for the lift," he called out as he alighted from the rear of the van.

"No problem!" Sonny replied.

"Deny everything!" the young man shouted. "Who loves ya, baby?" he roared as the van moved off.

To Rossa's relief, Sergeant Fogarty was leaving as he approached.

"There you are, Rossa," he remarked as he passed without stopping. "Investigations are continuing."

"What was that all about?" Rossa enquired as he stepped inside the mobile home.

His mother was trying to conceal her agitation.

"Nothing. Just a few details he needed to clear up."

"About the Nelson – "

"About various things. Where were you till now, anyway? Your lunch is cold."

"I told you – I was helping Lissy move her stuff."

"Well you should have been back before now. I have to go shopping with Rosaleen so you'll have to mind James."

"But I have soccer – "

"Oh, soccer now, is it? Your family comes last, I notice."

"Ah Mum – "

"You can bring James to soccer. Rosaleen's waiting for me!" She grabbed her coat and was gone before he could react. She was in one of those moods. Brilliant. James would have him at least twenty minutes late. He wolfed down the mince-and-mash without heating it.

"Come on, James. I'm in a hurry!" He half-dragged his brother along the road to Brennan's field.

Boy-Wonder Keeper Dropped! Liverpool boss Bill Shankly has sensationally dropped his boy-wonder keeper, Rossa Fox, on the eve of the FA Cup Semi-Final. "Disciplinary reasons," Shankly explained. "When you play for Liverpool, you play by my rules. If you don't turn up for training, you don't get on the team. Clemence is back in the team for Saturday."

"Sorry! I had to mind the wee fellow," Rossa explained to Gerry Brennan, who had stood in goals during Rossa's absence from the practice match.

"I'll let you off this time," Gerry warned in mock annoyance. "Get in here fast. I've let a goal in already. I was unsighted," he added quickly.

It wasn't one of Rossa's better performances either. He was distracted by James's wanderings about the field, by the visit of Sergeant Fogarty, by his mother's shortness with him. He was beaten by two more shots, one of which slid embarrassingly under his body.

"Defence was a bit on the slack side today," Gerry Brennan commented, eyeing Rossa deliberately. "We'll have to tighten up, boys. No training next Saturday and we all know why, don't we?"

"Yeh," a voice jeered. "Newcastle are going to wallop Liverpool in the Cup Final!"

"In your dreams, Billy Rogers, in your dreams!" Gerry retorted. "Right reason, wrong result! See you all in two weeks' time. Can I have a word, Rossa?"

Oh, oh, here it comes, Rossa thought. *Boy-wonder publicly humiliated by manager.*

"Well – are we going to win next Saturday?"

"Of course!" Rossa replied with relief.

"Would you like to see it on telly – with no distractions?" Gerry gave a knowing wink.

"Yeh – please!" Rossa cried.

"Pick you up at two! Try to be ready on time."

He walked home with a lighter heart. James enlivened the journey by pausing regularly to issue a stern warning.

"Get stuck in , will you. Get stuck in!"

There was no sign of Margie at Mass the following day. Rossa waited around in Lovely's in the hope that she might come in for the papers.

"You should be ashamed of yourself, selling that *News of the World*!" Beeny Flynn complained loudly. "Look at the cut of that hussy on the front page. Not a stitch on her."

"Lovely! Lovely! Lovely!" the distracted voice muttered from the other side of the counter.

"'Tis in my eye lovely! I don't see *The Irish Catholic* or the *Sacred Heart Messenger* here. I'll take a quarter pound of fruit bonbons. They're up there on the top shelf."

"Lovely! Lovely! Lovely!" The harassed shopkeeper began a search for the pole that would tip the fruit bonbons from the top shelf.

"I'm leaving the money for the *News of the World*," a voice called.

"Disgusting!" Beeny Flynn spat the word after the departing customer.

"Any chance of a glass of stout in here?" another voice shouted from the bar.

"I'm comin'! I'm comin'," Lovely replied as he struggled with the lid of the bonbon jar.

"Hiya, Foxie!" The voice startled Rossa. JJ had sidled up to his shoulder, accompanied by Paula.

"I hear you're suspect number one in the Nelson case," he leered. "You get twenty years for that around here. You can join Daddy in jail!"

"Come on, JJ. Get me a bottle of cider before my father comes looking for me," Paula said anxiously.

JJ limped up to the counter. Rossa noticed his foot was still in plaster. He noticed something else too. He hurried towards the door.

"Ah, throw in a couple more, let you," Beeny Flynn whined. "That's a very small quarter pound. Are you sure those scales are right?"

Rossa almost collided with Majella outside Lowney's.

"Is Paula coming?" she asked anxiously. "She made me wait here to keep an eye out for Daddy. Why do I always have to do her dirty work?"

"At the rate Lovely is going in there, she won't be out for an hour," Rossa replied.

"Well I'm not waiting round here for that long."

"I see she's back with JJ."

"Did you not hear? Bridie Doyle took a lift home from a disco with a fellow who had a mini. She told JJ she was fed up getting her bum frozen on his bike, so it's all off between them – and all on with Paula."

"Has he still got the bike?"

"Yeh. It's round the corner. You're not going to do anything to it?"

"No. Just curious."

He slipped around the corner to where JJ had parked the bike. He examined it carefully. Nothing on that side. He prised the bike away from the gable wall. Yes. Yes. One, two – three. Three spatters of yellow paint on the fork of the machine and on the wall of the tyre.

"Hey Rossa, wait for me," Majella called. "I'm not hanging round here any more."

He let the bike fall back against the wall. Three spatters of yellow paint on JJ's bike – and one on the plaster on his foot.

The boy-wonder keeper – dramatically recalled to the Liverpool team when Ray Clemence slipped on the stairs in the team's hotel room on the eve of the Cup Final – raced the length of the Wembley pitch. A penalty for Liverpool in the last minute and Bill Shankly had signalled to him to take it! A hush fell on the capacity crowd. JJ crouched on the Newcastle goal-line in his bright yellow sweater. He scowled at the boy-wonder, but Bill Shankly knew what he was about. The boy-wonder calmly cracked the ball to JJ's right as the keeper flung himself in the opposite direction.

Chapter Twenty-Two

Jim Daly drove Rossa and his mother to Drumroe School on Monday afternoon. Their appointment was for three o'clock. On the way Rossa told them of his suspicion of JJ.

"Did you tell Sergeant Fogarty?" Jim asked.

"No. I only saw the paint yesterday."

"Well I'll make it my business to see him this evening. I have no time for that JJ fellow. He's bad news. I wouldn't mind but I caught him chatting up Paula in Lowney's yesterday."

Rossa winced. Majella was in big trouble.

Jim dropped them at the school and drove away.

"How will we get home?" Rossa asked.

"Oh, we'll find a way," his mother replied with a faint smile.

Mr O'Connor welcomed them into his office. He was a tall, lean man of athletic build. Jim Daly had told Rossa that the principal was "a grand hurler in his day – played for the county." The sunshine reflected on his bald pate. Rossa had heard his cousins refer to him as Egg.

"Well, Rossa, what are your first impressions of this place?" His ability to switch from a warm smile to a stern frown unnerved Rossa.

"Seems OK," Rossa replied.

"Well, it's not the worst of schools. We like to think of it as one of the best, naturally. Fair play is our philosophy, Rossa. You play fair with us, we play fair with you. Which reminds me, do you play games?"

"Yeh. I play soccer – in goals."

"Hmmm." Mr O'Connor withdrew a sheet from a file and began to make notes on it. "And you have completed two years in –" he checked his file "– St Dominic's?"

"Yes."

"Two and a half, really," his mother corrected him.

"I see." Mr O'Connor quizzed him on the subjects he had studied in Belfast. He smiled, frowned, made notes and accepted comments from Rossa's mother. "And your cousins are the Dalys?"

"Yes."

"Hmmm. Majella is a grand girl. Good worker. We have our hands full with Paula, I'm afraid." He checked through his notes. In the silence Rossa could hear the sounds of school – sounds he had almost forgotten. An angry shout from a teacher, footsteps running down a corridor. A teacher calling out, "Walk, please!" Animated chat and laughter from a teacherless classroom. A basketball being bounced on the tarmacadam outside.

"Well now, Rossa. I think we can find a place for you in Drumroe in September."

The smile, then the frown.

"I suggest you start in second year. I don't think you'd manage the Inter Cert course in one year. Wouldn't be fair. And fair play is what we're about in Drumroe." The smile again. "How does that sound?"

"That sounds grand," his mother answered before Rossa could query the principal's offer.

No, it doesn't sound grand, he thought. Majella is in second year now. It's like starting in low babies.

Mr O'Connor slid back his chair and offered his hand to Rossa.

"You'll be welcome in Drumroe. Just play fair – and play a bit of hurling too! We need a few hurlers!"

He shook hands with Rossa's mother.

"By the way, our sports day is this day week. You're welcome to come along, Rossa, and get a feel of the place."

"That would be grand," his mother said.

Rossa bit his lip. Everything's grand when you don't have to do it.

They stood outside the front entrance.

"Now, how do we get home?" Rossa asked.

"On the school bus!" his mother replied.

"You must be joking!"

"No. I cleared it with Tom Farrell, the driver."

"But Mum – "

"Are you ashamed to be seen with me?"

"But, but mothers don't travel on school buses!"

"This one does!"

They sat in the front seats. Rossa could feel twenty pairs of eyes fixed on him, could hear their sniggers, imagine their gestures. He caught a glimpse of Paula hunched in a huge sulk in the back seat. Majella sat on her own. Just as the bus was about to move off, Margie came running from the school. She tumbled into the empty seats behind Rossa.

"I won't be offended if you want to move," his mother said. He slipped into the second seat. A chorus of whistles came from the rear of the bus. To hell with them, he thought.

"Hi! I thought you weren't at school. Didn't see you yesterday."

"We were in Dublin – looking at houses."

"Oh." He prised an imaginary thorn from his thumb. "About the slogans. I didn't – "

"I know that."

"I think I know who did – JJ."

"Surprise, surprise!"

He told Margie about Lissy's move. Suddenly the comments and jeers receded. The journey was all too short. They disembarked at Lowney's and walked down the Portabeg road. Maureen noticed the distinct coolness between the Daly sisters.

"Are you not talking to your sister, Paula?" she asked.

"She's not my sister. She's just a rat. A two-legged rat."

"Am not," Majella snapped. "Just because you were caught with JJ – "

"Who told on me? Rat! Jellyrat!"

"I'm sorry I asked," Maureen Fox sighed.

"I'm going to see Lissy on Wednesday," Rossa said. "Can you come?"

"Don't know," Margie said. "Depends."

Rossa nodded. He knew what it depended on.

"Sergeant Fogarty had a chat with JJ," Jim Daly told the Foxes on the following evening. "JJ got a bit of a shock but he denies he had anything to do with the slogans. Claims the paint on his bike must have come from driving over the paint spilled on the road. It's a bit of a stalemate at the moment."

"Michael Nelson should apologise to Rossa," Maureen said.

"There's nothing proven yet," Jim said, "so Rossa is still a suspect. Anyway, Michael Nelson is not the kind of man that would apologise too readily."

"Is he really moving because of the dump business?" Maureen asked.

"Who knows? He says it's because of his work. You never really get to know Michael Nelson. He's a strange man."

"What's the latest with the dump?"

"It's all over bar the shouting – and there won't be much of that! Lissy has been moved and the bulldozers are moving in on her old place next Monday. After that, they'll be dumping there in no time. Maybe we should all put up For Sale signs," he added with a resigned sigh.

James insisted on coming with Rossa to see Lissy.

"It's a longer journey now. You'll be tired!"

James was not to be put off.

"Chore! Chore! Chore!" he chanted.

Margie arrived, breathless, just as they were about to set off.

"Sorry! I had jobs to do. Daddy left a list before he went to Dublin."

It was nearly an hour later, after the inevitable pauses and coaxings with James, that they reached Lissy's. The builders were about to leave, having just completed the roof timbers of the house. Lissy was in a subdued mood. There were no records playing.

"Is everything all right?" Rossa asked.

"I spent the day looking for Siegfried," she sighed. "The old warrior has gone missing on me. He never settled here. I fear he may have come to grief, in his condition. I have only Butterfly left to me now. *Povera* Butterfly!"

James was delighted to find the pet lamb skipping around the enclosure in which the caravan was situated. Rossa and Margie left him there while they searched for Siegfried. Rossa gazed across the wide expanse of bog. It was pointless. Siegfried could be anywhere out there.

"He's gone to Valhalla, the home of the warriors," Lissy concluded. "No matter, I'll make us all a cup of tea. I'm an expert with the gas thing now, Rossa!"

She lit the gas ring to show off her expertise.

"I'm afraid I have no crisps for ye. Travelling Tom hasn't found my new abode yet. But there's soda bread . . ."

Rossa hadn't the heart to tell her of the proposed demolition of her old house. She had enough troubles for the moment. He remembered a record she had played for them on another occasion.

"I cannot bear the sad appearance of this place . . ."

"Are you running in the sports on Monday?" Rossa asked Margie on their return journey.

"Not if I can help it! I hate sports day."

"Why?"

"It's only for the show-offs who are good at sports. Then they tease and laugh at the rest of us who are no good. And Egg says everyone must take part in something."

"He invited me to come along."

"Are you coming?"

"No. I think I'll give it a miss. I might go up to see Lissy's old place being demolished. Do you want to come?" he asked jokingly.

Her answer surprised him.

"You never know! I might give the sports a miss too."

On the Thursday evening Rossa plucked up enough courage to put his "plan" to his mother.

"You what? Say that again! Are my ears playing tricks on me?"

"I – just thought I could finish out school in Belfast. I'd fit in better up there – "

"I don't believe this!" His mother lit a cigarette. "And where do you propose staying? In the Europa Hotel?"

"With Eileen Devlin – "

"Oh – so you've asked her?"

"I thought you might – "

"You did?" She drew furiously on the cigarette. "That was kind of you!"

"I could get a part-time job and pay her. Maybe send you some – "

"Oh, I see. You're going to be an airline pilot at the weekend. Sure you could fly down to Shannon with the shopping while you're at it!"

"Ah Mum – "

"Don't you 'Ah Mum!' me. Are you watching the telly? Reading the paper? They're slaughtering one another up there. The Loyalists are threatening to paralyse the province with a general strike. And you want to go back to that! As if we haven't suffered enough! I begged and crawled to get us out of there. I'm trying to make a life down here." Her voice was slowly breaking up. "And you want to go back? Over my dead body, Rossa Fox! Over my dead body!" She fumbled for another cigarette.

Rossa felt the walls closing in on him. He had to get outside. He picked up his football and made for the door.

"Don't just walk away, Rossa!" his mother called after him. "Face up to reality!"

He juggled the ball aimlessly around the patch of newly-cut grass outside the mobile home. Face reality? He was facing it.

Pluses – the soccer team, Gerry Brennan, Lissy . . .

Minuses – Margie leaving, her father's accusations, starting in a strange school in second year, JJ, two mocking cousins (who even now were squabbling in the kitchen of their house), James (maybe), his mother (definitely) . . .

Minuses win seven-three.

Boy-wonder keeper sensationally sent off! Fans howl with rage at referee who clearly did not see what happened . . .

"Rossa! Come here – at once! Quickly!" There was extreme urgency in his mother's voice. He strolled towards her.

"Quickly!" she snapped.

The news was on television.

"Now! Take a good look at that! A bomb in a pub in the Ormeau Road. Five dead and twenty or thirty injured. Maimed for life. Legs gone. Arms gone. That's your precious Belfast that you want to go back to . . ."

Rossa slumped onto the settee. There was nothing he could say.

Three-nil. Three beautiful goals to nil. Liverpool didn't

just win. They destroyed Newcastle. It was the one high point in a bad week.

"That was sweet!" Gerry Brennan said. "Very sweet indeed!"

He had taken Rossa to a hotel in Limerick where they watched the game in comfort and delight.

"And a victory like that has to be celebrated! What do you say to a big steak and chips?"

"I'd say Bill Shankly would approve!" Rossa replied.

"After you, Mr Clemence!" Gerry ushered him into the dining-room.

Over tea, Gerry outlined his plans for the soccer team.

"I'm hopeful we can organise a little league of our own for next season. Eight or ten teams. Might not be Division One, but it's a start!" He chewed on a mouthful of steak. "There's another thing. I'm thinking of making you captain of Portabeg United."

"I don't know if I'd be any good at that," Rossa replied. He was quite flattered by Gerry's proposal.

"Rubbish! You have the enthusiasm, the commitment and the knowledge. You know more about the game than the rest of them put together. So – it's agreed?"

"Thanks," Rossa said. He felt himself blushing all over.

"Now, I don't know about you," Gerry said, scanning the menu, "but banana fritters in chocolate sauce look like a winner to me."

Chapter Twenty-Three

A clinging mist hung over the top of Scroogawn as Rossa and James struggled to the top of the hill.

"Come on, James! We'll miss the big bulldozer! Get stuck in, James!" Rossa said, remembering his brother's most recently acquired phrase.

"Get stuck in, will you! Get stuck in!" James grunted.

"That's it!" Rossa laughed.

The mist had turned to a fine drizzle by the time they reached the top. There was no activity below them yet. Lissy's old house faced them. Beyond the house, Rossa could see the tops of two bulldozers.

I hope they start soon, he thought as he drew on the hood of James's anorak. Mum will murder me for getting us both drenched. A noise behind them startled him.

"You could have waited for me. Am I too late?" a breathless Margie panted.

Rossa was genuinely surprised to see her.

"Nothing's happened yet. Did you really mitch from school?"

"Sports day is bad enough. A rainy sports day is for the birds."

"Will you be in trouble at home?"

"Suppose so, if they find out." She looked away quickly and began to peer through the drizzle. "If they're going to do it, I wish they'd start. This is even worse than the sports."

As if in answer, a throaty roar came from one of the machines as it throbbed into action. The trio of spectators watched as the bulldozer charged, its huge blade biting like a giant jaw into the tin roof of the crumbling house. James put his hands over his ears to close out the grinding screech of metal on metal.

Margie crouched low and strained to peer into the fog of drizzle and demolition dust.

"Did you see something move down there?" she asked.

"Where?"

"In the doorway."

Rossa shielded the drizzle from his eyes. "There's nothing – "

The bulldozer attacked again, collapsing a section of the roof.

"There – again – at the door," Margie edged down the slope to get a better view.

This time Rossa could distinguish a moving blur in the doorway. It was more than a blur to Margie. It was the confused and frightened movement of an old and almost blind animal. Each time it came to the doorway, it seemed to stumble around in a circle and withdraw into the house again.

The bulldozer charged again.

Margie began to clamber down the side of Scroogawn.

"It's Siegfried!" she cried as she slithered and slid down to the level ground.

"No! Wait!" Rossa cried but Margie either could not or would not hear him.

She's crazy, he thought. The bulldozer will – He started down the slope after her.

"Get stuck in, will you! Get stuck in!" James cried as he began to follow him.

"No. Stay there, James," Rossa shouted but James was already tottering on a rock above him.

'Jesus, James! You're trouble wherever you go!" Rossa climbed back up, grabbed his brother around the waist and half-carried, half-dragged him down the slippery incline. James screamed in protest and began to pummel Rossa's head with his fists.

"Stop it!" Rossa roared, "or I'll just throw you in the ditch." James's weight and protest slowed his progress considerably.

Margie had reached the house but instead of going around to warn the bulldozer driver she went straight into the doorway in pursuit of Siegfried.

Rossa froze in horror as the bulldozer lumbered towards the house again.

The stupid – There was a terrifying crash as the chimney disintegrated and tumbled down on the surrounding roof which collapsed under its weight.

"No – !" Rossa screamed. He reached level ground, dropped James and began running towards the by-now roofless house. He hoped, prayed, he would see Margie come out of the house unscathed.

Nothing.

He paused, unsure of whether to go into the house or

around the back, but the grinding roar of the advancing bulldozer made the decision for him. He leapt over the paddock wall and tore around the side of the house, screaming and waving his arms.

The driver, intent on his work and wearing ear-muffs, was oblivious to Rossa's presence as he once more brought the huge blade down on the tangled mass of tin and timber. Rossa clamped his ears with his hands and howled in desperation. Only when he reversed his machine did the driver notice the sobbing figure sinking to his knees in the mud directly in his path.

The porch of Lissy's house was the only part that remained roofed. Rossa and the driver gaped at the problem that confronted them. A jagged tangle of twisted corrugated iron and broken timbers was piled to Rossa's height across the width of the kitchen. Rossa called out Margie's name. There was no response. Both he and the driver tore into the pile of debris simultaneously, pausing only to bark a warning to the curious James to keep well back as they flung sheets of iron or rotting beams behind them. The iron cut Rossa's hands but he ploughed through the debris, heedless, occasionally calling Margie's name. The drizzle made everything slippery but at least it kept the dust down.

Progress was slow. Rossa grew more fearful and cast anxious glances at the driver. James was screaming from behind the growing heap of rubble but he didn't care about James. Not now.

Suddenly the driver put his hand in the air in a gesture that called for silence. They paused. The driver pointed to his right. Was it a sound? The drizzle made it difficult to hear, not to mention James's bursts of protest. Rossa wanted to continue but the driver gestured again. They listened. Yes! The driver smiled. It was a tiny whimpering sound. It was Siegfried! They both wheeled to the right and burrowed furiously, creating a tunnel in the direction of the noise rather than attempting to remove the entire wall of rubble. The whimper grew louder. Rossa, being the smaller, felt his way into the tunnel. His fingers touched a quivering lump of matted hair. Siegfried! He moved his hand upwards. He felt a soaking woolly jumper. Margie! He nodded to the driver. They found a new energy, scooping and sweeping every obstacle to left and right. There at last was Margie's limp form crouched over a shaking Siegfried.

"Margie! It's OK. We're here!" Rossa cried. There was no response. The driver felt for a pulse.

"She's alive, but unconscious. It may be best not to move her. Just clear more stuff away. I'll go for help. Can you manage?"

Rossa nodded.

"I'll bring the little fellow with me – "

"No. He – he won't go with you. Just lift him in here – but please go quickly!"

James began to stroke Siegfried.

"Chore! Chore! Chore!" he whispered.

Rossa looked about him in disbelief. The whole thing was crazy. The three of them caught in the debris of Lissy's house where they had spent so many happy times. He looked down at Margie's chalk-white face.

"Don't die on me, please!" He began to sob. "Don't die! You're my best friend! Please!" He suddenly found himself in an angry mood. Angry with Margie.

"What did you have to do a stupid thing like that for?

Stupid! Stupid! Stupid!" he cried. The rain was washing the mud from Margie's hair.

"Here," Rossa whispered. He tore off his anorak and spread it over her body. "Just hold on! They'll be here soon."

A memory of a piece of paper floated across his rain-drenched eyes.

I am a good girl. I am a good girl.

"Please don't die!" he croaked. "They'll be here soon."

It seemed like an eternity before he heard the welcome sound of an ambulance siren wailing across the bog.

"Easy now! Easy!" the ambulance-man called to his colleague as they lifted Margie onto a stretcher. They stumbled across the rubble to the ambulance and quickly laid the stretcher inside.

"How about you, son?" the ambulance man asked.

"I'm – we're OK. She was the only one trapped. Along with him." He motioned towards the dog in his arms.

"I'll look after them, boys." Rossa noticed Sergeant Fogarty for the first time. "Come on, Rossa," he said, "I'll take you home."

"We have to bring – Siegfried – home to Lissy." Rossa's voice was reduced to a hoarse whisper. He suddenly felt very cold. The ambulance moved off, its beacon illuminating the gathering gloom as the rain grew heavier. Please, he prayed. Rossa slid into the back seat of the squad car. For the second time in a short while, he left Lissy's house in a police car after a traumatic experience.

"I'll look after the dog," Sergeant Fogarty said. "It's home first for you two."

The rest of the day was a blur to Rossa. A hot bath

revived him in Rosaleen's house before an angry tearful mother burst in, fearful of what to expect. She cradled James's head in her arms while berating Rossa.

"Is there no end to this? I never know what you're up to. Putting this child's life in danger – "

"Leave him, Maureen," her sister pleaded. "He's had a rough time."

"All I know is," his mother sobbed, "I'll be glad when he goes to school. At least I'll know where he is . . ."

Rosaleen put her arm around Rossa.

"She's just frightened and upset," she whispered. For once, Paula and Majella were subdued, genuinely worried as they all waited for news of Margie.

Late in the evening Jim Daly brought that news.

"She's regained consciousness. Broken arm, cuts, bruises, some internal injuries, a lot of shock – but she'll pull through. She'll be all right!" he announced.

There were murmurings of "Thanks be to God" from the assembled group. In his mind's eye Rossa saw Margie's chalk-white face turn to a shy smile as he drifted into a deep sleep.

Chapter Twenty-Four

Sergeant Fogarty pressed the doorbell a third time before Michael Nelson opened the door.

"Sorry, Sergeant. It's – Jesus, is it bad news?"

"No. Margie's holding her own. Can we come in?"

"Of course. Of course. In to the left – Angela's there."

Sergeant Fogarty nodded to Mrs Nelson who sat in an armchair, twisting and turning a hankie through her fingers.

"Sit down, please." Michael Nelson motioned towards the settee.

"This is Dr Maura Walsh from the hospital," Sergeant Fogarty explained.

"Is Margie – ?" Mrs Nelson began.

"She's doing grand," Dr Walsh reassured her.

Sergeant Fogarty took out a notebook and cleared his throat.

"I'll explain why Dr Walsh is here. As you know, Margie has some internal injuries. In the course of examining those injuries –" He hesitated. "I'll let Dr Walsh explain."

"In the course of treating Margie," Dr Walsh began, "we came across marks that were not consistent with her accident in the bog – "

"For God's sake, what are you saying?" an agitated Michael Nelson snapped.

"Upon further investigation," Dr Walsh continued, "we have established that Margie has been the victim of abuse of both a physical and sexual nature over – "

"You mean she has been – interfered with?" Michael Nelson interrupted again.

"That is so."

Angela Nelson began to cry quietly.

"It's that pup down the road. That young Provo. I knew he was trouble," Michael Nelson shouted. "She should never have – have you charged him?" He turned to Sergeant Fogarty.

"We haven't and we won't be," Sergeant Fogarty replied calmly. "Margie has told us the entire story."

Angela Nelson was now sobbing loudly.

"What do you mean, 'the entire story'?" Michael Nelson began fidgeting with his fingers. "For God's sake, Angela . . ." he appealed to his wife.

"I think you know very well what the entire story is," Sergeant Fogarty replied. "Serious charges have been made against you and I have to caution you at this stage that anything you say may be taken down as evidence . . ."

Michael Nelson initially affected shock and disbelief until the whispering voice of his wife intruded on the silence.

"It's true . . . It's true . . . It's true," she repeated.

"Shut up, Angela," her husband snapped. "This is all –

all – all – " His voice trailed away as his head sank slowly into his hands.

Rosaleen Daly shook her head.

"I just can't believe that – that this was going on and none of us suspected anything. I mean I used to admire Michael Nelson for all the work he did for the community."

"I never liked him," her sister said. "I was never at ease with him. And he certainly never liked us. He had it in for poor Rossa from the start. He just stooped so low . . ."

Maureen Fox had also had a visit from Sergeant Fogarty.

"The minute you showed me that anonymous note, I knew I had seen that notepaper before. It was a peculiar shade of blue. It took a while before I remembered where I had seen it – in Michael Nelson's file on the dump protest. I managed to get a few pages of it from him recently. Identical! Same watermark. He was a very stupid man making a mistake like that. He might as well have signed his name to the letter . . ."

"The poor devil!" Jim Daly remarked. "You'd be inclined to feel sorry for him. I mean, it's thought now that he might have painted the slogans on his own wall. The man was clearly troubled – "

"For crying out loud, Jim!" Maureen Fox broke in. "The man was clearly twisted! To do that to his own daughter, ruining her life. He should be locked up for good. And how his wife put up with it all – "

"Seems he had them all terrorised," Rosaleen said. "Who knows what goes on behind closed doors, anywhere."

"I don't care," Maureen disagreed. "She should have

stood up to him." She lit another cigarette and paused to glance at the television news that played in the background. "Just like someone should stand up to them strikers in the North. The place is in chaos. To think that Rossa wanted to go back to *that*!"

"How is he taking all of this – about Margie?" Rosaleen asked.

"I don't know. You never know with teenagers – and you certainly never know with him."

Rossa sat at the foot of a pine-tree in Portabeg Wood. It was a warm, humid day. He savoured the cool of the pine wood. The scent of pine hung heavily in the air.

He withdrew a copybook from his jeans pocket and attempted to smooth the folds out of the pages. He picked up the pen which had been clipped onto the copybook and began to write.

Dear Margie,

Hi! It's me. I don't know if you'll ever get this letter but I'm writing it anyway.

It's hot. I'm sitting out in the wood writing this. Just to be away from people. You know.

I hope you're feeling better. Uncle Jim says you'll be staying with your aunt in Ennis when you get out of hospital. I hope you'll come back here later on. Life is pretty miserable with my two mad cousins.

I can't write about what happened to you. I want to but I can't. I just want to say I understand about you writing, "I am a good girl." I didn't then. I do now. I want to KILL your father. Knife him, strangle him, shoot him. The Bastard. The Bastard. I want to tear him apart . . .

His hand shook terribly. The tears rolled on to the page and smudged his writing. He ripped the page out of the copybook and then proceeded to tear the page viciously into the tiniest shreds possible.

Jim Daly drove Rossa and James to Moneen. It was Rossa's first visit to Lissy's since the accident.

"A Dhia na trócaire, that poor girl. How is she?" Lissy cried on greeting them.

"She's coming along grand," Jim replied. "She'll be fine."

"I was out of my mind with worry for her. I could find no one to tell me how she was. And to think she did it all for old Siegfried."

"How is he?" Rossa asked.

"Ah, just in it. His wandering days are over. He'll not last much longer. I'm just sorry he caused so much trouble."

"Don't fret about it, Lissy," Jim said. "Anyway, James has something for you, haven't you, James?"

"Go on, James," Rossa prompted, pointing to the back seat of the car. James moved slowly, to Rossa's irritation. He eventually emerged with a collie pup cradled in his arms.

"You have to give it to Lissy," Rossa hissed but James remained totally engrossed in the squirming bundle of fur in his arms. "It's for you whenever James decides to hand it over," Rossa sighed.

"The *coileán* is for me?" Lissy gazed at the pup in disbelief.

"You can thank Uncle Jim," Rossa said. "He saw the ad

in the *Clare Champion* – 'Collie pups free to good homes.' It's to replace Pinkerton."

"*Grazie! Grazie!*" Lissy whispered as she stroked the pup's furry coat.

"It's a present from all of us," Rossa explained.

"A present? When did anyone ever give me a present?" Lissy mused aloud. "Ye'll have a cup of tea or something," she announced suddenly. "And I have crisps! Travelling Tom was here at last!"

"Crips! Crips! Crips!" James cried excitedly as he handed the pup to Lissy.

Chapter Twenty-Five

"Come on, Rossa! Today's the day!"

Rossa burrowed under the blankets away from his mother's cheery voice.

"Up and at them!" The blankets were stripped back.

"Ah Mum!" he cried. He glanced at his watch. Ten past seven! When had he last got up at ten past seven?

Actually he could answer that question. It was the morning they left Belfast. He could still hear his mother panicking. "For God's sake, Rossa. Will you get a move on! Barney's going to be here at half seven." Was it really six months ago? Or six lifetimes?

Pins. Why were there so many pins in a new shirt? And no matter how many you picked out, you always missed one. He smelled the newness of the white shirt. It reminded him of First Communion Day . . .

"Ah Rossa, look what you've done to your lovely new shirt!" his mother cried. "What are you laughing at?" she snapped at her husband. His father, sitting across from Rossa in the restaurant, was shaking with laughter. Rossa looked disconsolately at the big blob of chocolate ice cream sliding down the front of his shirt. He began to laugh also. His mother tried in vain to scrape off the ice cream with a spoon. "Well ye might laugh," his mother sighed. "Ye don't have to wash this and get rid of the stain!"

"Don't forget, Maureen," Patrick Fox chuckled. "Persil washes whiter!" He gave a big wink to his son . . .

"Hurry, Rossa! Your breakfast is ready!"

He pulled on the green jumper and felt the crest on the front . . .

Boy-Wonder Keeper Gains First Irish Cap. Rossa Fox, the boy-wonder keeper, now firmly established at Liverpool, has been rewarded with a first cap for Ireland. After a brilliant season with Liverpool, Fox will pull on the No. 1 jersey tonight for Ireland's friendly with Brazil . . .

He slung the almost-empty bag over his shoulder. There were tears in his mother's eyes.

"Come on! Give me a big hug!"

"Ah Mum. Paula and Majella are watching!"

"Let them! This reminds me of your first day at St Dominic's. I bawled my eyes out all day!"

"Well don't start now!" He disentangled himself from his mother's hug. "See you! See you, James. Good luck at school." James made no reply.

"Come on, Rossa!" Majella called. "You'll have us all late!"

He followed them up the road to Lowney's Cross. They made half-hearted attempts to involve him in their conversation but invariably that conversation centred on themselves.

"Jelly, on no account are you to let JJ know I was out with Frankie Lyons last night – "

"I couldn't be bothered!"

"Well just watch what you say – or else I'll tell Seamus Dunne about the poem you wrote about him!"

"Paula Daly – you went through my private things!"

"I wouldn't say behind the Sacred Heart picture is private, Jelly!"

The protest signs still lined the road to Lowney's Cross – some broken, some weathered, some askew – but still there, in defiance of the lorries that rumbled across the bog each week to the newly-opened dump at Scroogawn. Mary Roarty had tried to reorganise the Protest Committee but her efforts were fruitless. The Portabeg community had accepted the inevitable. Hurl them, Portabeg . . .

They reached Lowney's. Twenty past eight. There were two other students sitting on the window-sill of the shop window.

"The bus doesn't come until half-eight," Majella announced.

"You told me twenty past," Rossa said.

"That was just to get you here on time."

A sudden breeze whipped up the sweet-wrappers and crisp-packets that had collected in the shop doorway. Rossa watched the paper scraps chase each other around in circles . . . A sheet torn from a copy book danced before his eyes. I am a good girl . . . I am a good girl . . . He winced.

Michael Nelson had not been seen in Portabeg since his secret was exposed. There was talk of a court case in November. The Nelson house was sold but still unoccupied. Margie and her mother had returned to the area and were renting a small house. Rossa had only met her twice since her return. The first meeting had been awkward, tentative.

I am a good girl . . . I am a good girl . . .

They had spoken little and about other things – Lissy, Siegfried, James.

The second meeting was at Lissy's. Lissy became very distressed on seeing Margie and held her hand for the entire duration of the visit.

"And after all your trouble, the old warrior died on me last week. He's gone to the Valhalla at last," Lissy said. "But I have the *coileán* – and a lovely *coileán* he is too. Pinkeen I call him. When he grows up he'll be Pinkerton!"

When they were leaving, Lissy placed her hand on top of Margie's head and began to sing gently.

"Un bel di vedremo . . ."

On the way home, Rossa noticed an ease in Margie that had not been there on the journey to Lissy's.

The school bus swung around the bend and slowed up as it approached Lowney's. Rossa tightened his grip on the bag strap and swung it nervously to and fro. This was it. The moment he dreaded.

The others charged to the door of the bus and whooped greetings to the occupants inside. Rossa slid into the front seat, hoping not to be noticed by the others in their excitement.

"Sit down, let ye!" Tom Farrell roared. "Ye're like a herd of mountain goats."

The bus was about to pull out when a small blue car drove across its path. Tom Farrell swore at the driver who waved in apology to him. The passenger door opened. It was Margie!

She clambered aboard the bus muttering "Sorry" to Tom and sat beside Rossa. The effect on the gabbling crowd at the back of the bus was electric. Total silence. Rossa could imagine them collectively holding their breaths. Tom Farrell began to whistle nervously as the bus moved off.

"Am I glad to see you!" Rossa whispered.

"Mum offered to drive me to school but I asked to go on the bus," Margie replied, slightly breathless. "Have to face it some time. Better on the first day. Anyway, I was thinking you would need company too."

It was the "too" that thrilled Rossa. He was lost in admiration of her.

"Don't – mind – me," he stammered. "You're very – brave. I've dreaded this day for months but you – must –"

She turned slightly and gave a weak smile.

"We need each other," she said.

We – need – each – other. The four most beautiful words he had ever heard.

Boy Wonder Keeper Holds Jules Rimet Trophy Aloft . . .

Rossa Fox, the boy wonder keeper holds up the trophy before a sea of adoring fans as Ireland sensationally wins the World Cup following a last-minute penalty save . . .

He slid further into his seat, conscious of the rising buzz of chatter from the back of the bus.

"Look at the length of Jamesie Larkin's hair! Egg is going to send you straight home, Jamesie!"

Another voice impersonated the school principal.

"Did you sleep through the shearing season, Mr Larkin?" Laughter.

"Hey, did you hear Frankie Lyons is coming back? He stuck the Leaving Cert and he's going to repeat!"

"That'll make Egg happy! He'll have him back on the hurling team!"

"Not half as happy as Caroline Smith!" More laughter.

Rossa closed his eyes and smiled.

Don't, Majella, he thought. Please don't even open your mouth . . .

Glossary of Irish words and phrases

anois	now
anseo!	here!, present!
a stór	my love
buachaill cneasta	a kind boy
carn	a heap, a pile
coileán	a puppy
créatúirín	little creature
a chréatúirín	o little creature
go bhfóire Dia orainn!	God help us!
gread!	move!
in ainm Dé	in the name of God
leaba Laoise	Laoise's bed
peata	pet
scuit!	scram! Get out of here!
tine	fire
tóg é!	take it!
uainín	a little lamb
uainín eile ar strae	another little lost lamb

Note:

Chore and *forish* are meaningless expressions used to calm and coax animals.

Glossary of Italian words and phrases

addio	farewell
andiamo	let's go
arrivederci	goodbye
attenti!	attention!
bellissima	beautiful one
bene	good! Well done!
buon giorno!	good day!
che bella giornata!	what a lovely day!
che sfortuna!	bad luck to it!
ciao!	hi!, hello!
grazie!	thanks!
i miei cari amici	my dear friends
la gelosa	the jealous one
la traviata	the fallen woman
le mie canzoni	my songs
o mio piccolo tesoro	oh my little lamb
presto!	quickly!
speriamo bene	let's hope for the best
vieni!	come!

Operatic lines and phrases

addio, fiorito asil	farewell, flowery refuge
bel nome	a pretty name
bimba, bimba non piangere	don't cry, my child
povera Butterfly	poor Butterfly

santo Dio!	holy God!
tienti la tua paura	keep your fears to yourself
un bel di vedremo	one fine day we'll see
levarsi un fil di fumo	a wisp of smoke rising
vedi? Egli é venuto?	you see? He has come!
vissi d'arte, vissi d'amore	Love and music, these
	have I lived for (Tosca)